Rockhaven WEDDING

Farley Dunn

●♦● THREE SKILLET

ROCKHAVEN WEDDING, Dunn, Farley L

First Edition

A Katie Carver Novel

 THREE SKILLET

www.ThreeSkilletPublishing.com

v.2

ISBN 978-1-943189-04-5

Enjoy all the Katie Carver novels:

Rockhaven Summer

Rockhaven Wedding

Rockhaven Christmas

Rockhaven Spring

Author's Note

Those of you familiar with Mid-Coast Maine will recognize elements of Vinalhaven Island in my Rockhaven series, but only because of my family history and the summers I've spent there. If you do visit Vinalhaven someday, look for Rockhaven. You'll find that magical place strewn all about the craggy shoreline and in the stalwart people that call Vinalhaven home.

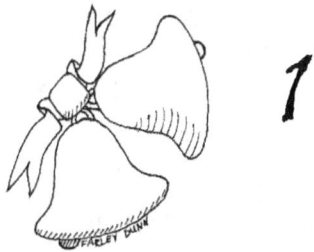

1

Katie Carver's delicate fingers flew across her keyboard. She typed with immaculately manicured nails, the black letters appearing out of nowhere, blocky and dark, and they glistened when they caught in the wind.

Caught in the wind?

She smiled and closed her eyes, aware how silly that was, letters caught in the wind. Instead she pictured a sailboat with the words Lil' Dude neatly painted on the back, the ocean off a Maine island, and catching the wind with a sail humming in the stiff breeze. The picture was complete with Jeff Ragsdale at her side, as he had been just weeks before.

She shook her head and pulled her hands from her keyboard. She knew one thing. Her letters had better not catch in the wind, not if she was to get her deadlines met. Yet, at the same time, she wanted them to do exactly that. She pulled a single sheet of paper from a chrome-plated letter tray on her desk, one containing a printed email from Jeff. She stroked the words gently with the fingertips of one hand. The black ink spoke her fiancé's love carried across two hundred miles of wire and cable, sent from Jeff to her. These were the words she wanted to catch in the wind.

Her thoughts of Jeff were interrupted by something a little less endearing.

"Katie? Are you awake this morning? You have a call on Line 3." A trimly dressed woman holding a company-issued black tablet stood at the entrance to Katie's cubicle. She leaned one elbow casually over the low cubicle wall.

"Oh!" Katie laughed guiltily. There her phone was, blinking red on Line 3. "Sorry, Connie. I was distracted."

"Dear, you deserve to be distracted. You've other things on your mind besides minivans and SUVs. Better get that call, though." She winked, and she pointed at the phone.

Connie was Connie Rivera, Claims Specialist for ALDMass, the fastest-growing discount auto insurer in New England. Auto Liability Discount was on the letterhead, but say "Old" Mass, and it was instant brand recognition. *Stability is our middle name.* Well, actually, Liability was the company's middle name, but the ads worked. They were the fastest growing in New England, after all.

Connie was Katie's immediate supervisor.

"Katie Carver, Old Mass Claims Department. How may I assist you?"

"Come to Rockhaven for the weekend?"

Katie looked up at Connie, still hovering over her wall, to see her smiling broadly. "Told you you better get that call." She turned and stepped away with a brief wave.

"Oh, Jeff, I miss you so much. I want to. I so want to, but Fridays are tough. Especially this Friday." And she did want to go. After the week so recently spent on the island, and finding that the daring and adventuresome boy she'd loved years before still waited on her, coming home had been the most difficult thing she'd ever done.

"What's there for you?" His words laughed without laughing. "After all, I'm here."

She pictured him as she spoke, his dimples crinkling, or the wind in his flyaway island hair on his lobster boat, and the completely different man who donned clerical robes and lovingly guided Rockhaven Town Church's members and attendees past life's rocky ledges. Yes, she wanted to be there.

Or him to be here.

"Think you can make Friday's 2:45 ferry? If not, I can make the 10:30."

She sighed, shaking her head. He knew better. For her to make the 2:45 meant a crack-of-dawn exit from Boston, and Jeff on the 10:30? With city traffic, he was getting to Boston about midnight. Then to turn around and return? He couldn't miss Sunday services.

"I heard that sigh, Dame Carver. Does that mean

you're turning me down?"

"I really thought I could just walk away." From her Boston life, she meant. *Hoped* was a better word. *Wanted to* was also pretty accurate. Old Mass had to hire a replacement, and there was paperwork to file, retirement accounts to settle, and that was just with her job. Her apartment lease and her car? She hadn't had time to think about those.

"What can you not walk away from? I miss you, Katie. A lot. I get you for a week, and you disappear again. Phone calls aren't enough." He chuckled, but it sounded like his throat caught. Like there was more emotion there than he was willing to show. "I can't hold you or smell your hair over the phone. One Friday. This Friday. That's all I ask."

"If only I could. I'm one of the principal presenters. I can't just not be here." Getting in the way this Friday were the Old Mass regional reps from across New England who would be gathering at ALDMass' Boston headquarters. The meetings had been in the works for months.

"You're breaking my heart, Dame Carver." He teased her again. "I had hoped. That's all. Maybe next weekend?"

"Jeff, you're going to make me cry if you keep on. You know the office has a shower planned next Friday. They want you here, but I explained about the ferry, and you having to be back for Sunday services." She said that to show him she cared, that even in this, she was watching out for him.

"I'm off the hook, huh?" He didn't sound like he

wanted to be off the hook.

"I got your email." She pulled out the paper from earlier, touching it lovingly. It was a distraction from the weekend's discussion, and she knew it. Still, the email had touched her, all ten times she'd read it.

"You did, huh?" His grin came through in his words.

"How long did it take?" To sail around East Haven Island, she meant. Jeff would get that. He'd mentioned it in the letter.

"You know how fast the Dude is."

"I know how big East Haven is. What about the tide?" Again, half said, understanding the shared thoughts better than most couples understood a whole discussion.

"Might've scraped a board or two."

"Jeff. Don't tease." Hearing him talk about the Dude, the twelve-foot catboat she'd learned to sail at nine, made turning down his offer especially hard. He had it there. She didn't have it here. There was nothing easy in that.

"Gotta tempt you with something. Is the 2:45 sounding pretty good, yet?"

"It sounds too wonderful to imagine. I want to be there, but this is real life. Six weeks, and I can be there all the time. I can't do it any faster. I'm so sorry."

"I love you, Dame Katie. I'll be thinking of you every minute. I'll call you at home tonight."

"You'd better. I love you, too, Reverend Jeff."

Placing the phone back in its cradle, Katie gave her heart a minute to settle. Being separated from Jeff again after thinking she had lost him for fourteen years was one of the hardest things she had ever forced herself to do.

In addition, there was one more thing. She had a wedding to plan, and there were fifteen miles of ocean in the way. She could only hope she didn't drown somewhere along the way.

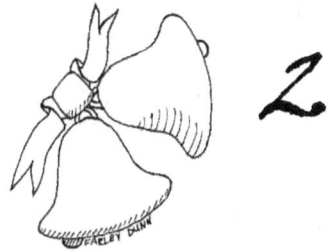

2

"What's this?"

Half the office staff blocked Katie's way out. She had shut down her computer, and for the first time in days, she thought she might actually get out of the building on time.

"What's what?" The reply was more a giggled tease than a real answer, and it came from Ashlynn Seabourn, a thin blonde with tightly curled hair.

"Eight of you hovering around my cubicle like summer butterflies around a stand of milkweed." At the five o'clock notification bell, office personnel normally evaporated like sea mist in the sunshine, and Katie had hoped to be one of them.

"We have something for you."

That was sung in chorus by two sisters who had worked on the Old Mass insurance circuit before

ALDMass had become Old Mass. They looked less like sisters than friends who had similar tastes in jewelry and makeup. Isabelle Lawton was the elder, short, dark, and round; while her sister Lesly Buchannan was trim and svelte. One was married, but Katie had trouble remembering which. Lesly, she thought.

"What?" Katie shook her head. It was now after five.

"This!" River Sopko, a dark-haired petite Asian beauty waved a card in the air. Katie's name was in bold print on the front.

"That's sweet of you." For this, she didn't mind being trapped. Not as much, anyway. She reached for it.

"No, not so fast." River pulled the card away.

"Friday's!" The final four women sang out the name of the iconic restaurant in four-part harmony. Lisa Vickers sported long, Cher-like tresses. Kambri Green peered through ever-present gold wire frames. Michelle Jeter matched Kambri's wires, except she wore her gold in great hoops in her ears. Ellie Reese's signature was an old-fashioned pageboy that gave her a cuttingly contemporary look.

"I can't." Katie laughed with them, but she didn't have time to spend an entire evening out on the town. Especially tonight. Jeff was calling.

"Oh, yes, you can." Michelle in her hoops pulled the group's trump card out of her purse. "Look what we have!"

It was a key ring with a large, yellow smiling face attached. Katie's key ring.

"How . . ." Katie opened her purse, to find hers missing, only to hear Ellie tease her.

"How many sets of keys do you keep in there, because we have one."

"How did you get them? I've had my purse with me all day."

"*Almost* all day. Connie's such a team player. Remember that emergency report she had you run to her?" Isabelle looked smug. "I was right outside your cubicle, and I waved to you. Remember?"

"Izzy, and I thought you were my friend." Katie wagged her finger at her.

"And Lisa's friend, and River's friend, and Kambri's friend—"

"I get it." Katie grabbed her arm, laughing. "You don't need to name everyone here."

"Oh, but I do!" Isabelle was in full swing by then, pointing around Katie to the other women. "And Ellie and Michelle and Lesly and Ashlynn. There. Got 'em all."

"I have my husband's van today!" Lesly shook a set of keys attached to a dark leather fob, the sort a man would carry. "It's a surprise wedding shower! We're stealing you away for the evening. Off to Brookline!"

"I tried for the Dedham Friday's on Boston Providence Highway. It would be less crowded, but who cares! Party!"

Katie wasn't sure who said that, but by then, they were tumbling out the door into the late July heat, and into the parking garage. It was Fenway that might be the problem. They'd be driving right past. This was the city. Catch game-night traffic, and they'd add at least an hour to their drive time.

At least she had her cell. If the events of the evening went on too long, she could text Jeff and let him know where she was. Yet, right then, she could barely hang onto her purse. She had eight friends, all excited as summer magpies, strong-arming her to a waiting van to cart her off across the city.

They survived the van ride, making it to Friday's in record time, although four had to crowd the last seat. Lesly pulled to the door and shooed the rest out, offering to go and park the van. Isabelle took Katie's purse and dropped it in an underseat bin.

"No, you don't." She waggled her finger at Katie. "You don't need any money, and we won't have anyone calling for a taxi. You're all ours tonight. No distractions allowed."

Katie shouldn't have been surprised to find they were expected, and a large table was set up for them. There were balloons, streamers, and even flowers in the middle of the table. It was Connie Rivera that made sense of it all.

"Did you guess at any time today, my dear?" Connie took Katie's hands and led her to the seat of honor. "We've been planning this since the first day we heard of you leaving us. Oh, we are going to be so sad you're gone." She patted the sides of Katie's face, and she had red rings around her eyes.

"Oh, I do love you so much, Connie." Katie threw her arms around her supervisor.

"Then stay." Connie pushed her away and held her at arm's length, looking hard in her eyes.

"Connie! Connie!" Katie didn't know what to say to that.

"I'm teasing. A good man is so much better than a good job." Connie squeezed her hands and motioned for her to sit. "Now, Katie, we've taken up an envelope to cover tonight, so you order whatever you want. Don't even look at the prices. Tonight is our treat."

Katie laughed when Connie handed her a menu. It had been prepared beforehand with all the prices taped over with blue painter's tape.

They had a waiter and a waitress step up and seat everyone else, and within minutes, menus were in everyone's hand. Tea and sodas appeared, with water for Isabelle, and coffee for Connie.

The ladies had prepared special cards, and each one stood, reading, singing, or acting out their written sentiments. Katie laughed and cried, sometimes at the same time, as she reconnected with remembered events, joys, and experiences shared with those around her.

River reminded everyone of her brother, visiting from Vietnam, now married, but once a blind date for Katie. It had been a disaster, with raw seafood that Katie claimed had climbed off her plate.

Ashlynn told of her mother's illness, and long talks with Katie, who understood because of the way her grandmother died.

Izzy and Lesly had never traveled abroad, and Katie had borrowed the money for them to go, never expecting it to be returned. It had become the down payment on her new car.

Kambri was her Saturday lunch date on cold, winter weekends. Katie had kept Lisa's bird on more than one occasion. Michelle's latest boyfriend had been suggested by Katie.

Ellie? They wore the same iridescent Brandywine nail polish, often borrowing from one another at work.

The evening slipped into small gifts opened, and that card held so high by tiny River? It was much more than just a card.

This was the real wedding shower, they hooted and called out, waving the card in the air before turning it over to her. The shower planned the next week at work would be a meet-and-greet. Cake and cookies. Just another boring shower for the boring crowd. The juicy stuff was coming tonight.

Of course, they were teasing about the upcoming shower at ALDMass, but they were serious about one thing. That card? It was a generous gift certificate to a high-end boutique, one aimed directly at the honeymoon crowd. When Katie opened that, the entire group erupted into hooting catcalls, and even more fun was had by all.

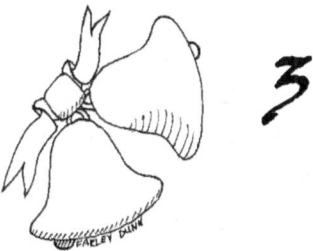

3

"**I** need my purse!" Katie had enjoyed the meal, but it was well past Jeff's time to call, and now she felt guilty. Her phone was in her purse, and her purse was in the front seat.

"No, no! You go in the back!" Ellie and River jostled her into the rear seat. "That purse isn't going anywhere."

"Why are you doing this to me?" Katie saw her purse out and tried for it. She really did, but she was trapped by her coworkers, and within minutes, they were headed down the street to drive the most impossible roadways in the state. She was laughing, but she knew how close she was to tears. "I need my purse. My phone's inside."

"Here. Take mine. I get free nationwide minutes, even off shore." It was Kambri.

19

"Yeah. *Off shore.*" Several voices chimed in, and in the glow of the interior lights and occasional passing street lamp, it was impossible to tell just who it was. However, it was clear just what they meant. She could call *Jeff,* and they could listen in to every word.

"Okay. I give in." Katie took the phone with a chuckle, her palms already sweaty. Some of it was anticipation. Behind that was the guilt. She'd known he was going to call, and yet she had let her friends pull her away for a night on the town, having fun, doing all the city things she would no longer be able to do on the island. Calling Jeff was like turning the Boston switch off and shutting her friends out of the life that would soon be hers.

Or shutting herself out of the busy city life that she'd come to love as part of who she was.

At this particular moment, surrounded by these particular friends, she didn't want to let go of her stimulating city life. Rather, she did, but she was aware of exactly how much she'd come to depend on her friends and how much each one meant to her. It would be hard. Very hard.

"How do I turn this on?" Katie tapped the flat panel and only got a pattern of dots that quickly faded away once again.

"Oh, here." Kambri tilted the phone her direction and traced her finger in a pattern, then pushed it back to Katie. "Just punch in the numbers and hit call."

"Hit call, girl!" Izzy and Lesley tittered and clapped wildly.

She typed in the first six numbers, and the last

four, well, who could forget J-E-F-F? It wasn't really JEFF, but that's how she remembered them. 8-6-6-6 were the numbers just under J-E-F-F.

"Is it ringing?" Ashlynn pushed the phone to Katie's ear. "I know what I hear. Two little lovebirds, sitting in a tree. K-I-S-S-I-N-G. First comes—"

"Shush! He's picking up." Katie held her finger to her lips. She giggled, feeling stupid, and yet not feeling stupid at all. It was her friends huddled around listening, and the apology she knew she needed to make. It was finding the words she must choose to explain not being at her phone that twisted her stomach just the tiniest amount.

What she heard was not what she expected.

"Jeff Ragsdale. I'm either away from the phone; doing the Lord's work; or my battery's gone dead. Whichever, leave a message. You'll hear from me ASAP." Then the line beeped. Katie frowned and looked up, totally off kilter. That was one thing she had not expected.

"What did he say?" River waved her hand in front of Katie's face. "Wake up, there. He said something, or you wouldn't have that look on your face."

"He said I should leave a message."

"I can do that for you!" Kambri grabbed the phone. "Kissy, kissy, Jeff!" With a wink, she pursed her lips and made several kissing sounds, and then she dramatically tapped the off button and dropped the phone in her purse.

"Oh, Kambri, you are so wicked!" Ashlynn was wiping her eyes by that time, she was laughing so hard.

"Wicked good! That's me, wicked good!" Kambri fluffed the ends of her hair as if primping. "Since Jeffie's not home, we have more hours to kill."

"Whoo, whoo," Lesly called out, starting up the van. "My husband's out for hours, yet. Where to, girls?"

"A movie! Let's go see a movie!" Ellie and River chanted together. "Brad Pitt! Brad Pitt!"

"Somebody younger!" That was Isabelle, with a petulant look on her face.

"Oh, Izzy, not a Jonas brothers' movie. You're not a tweener anymore, so I forbid you to see even one additional tween heartthrob flick. So, there." Lesly waggled her hand over the seat, pointing to her sister, as if that were it, and she'd not hear another word about it.

Katie didn't want a Jonas movie, and she had no desire to see anything else, either. That phone call bothered her. How could Jeff not have picked up? He always picked up. It had been twelve hours since she'd spoken with him, and his words reminded her of how dependable he was: *I'll be thinking of you every minute. I'll call you at home tonight.*

And she hadn't had her phone to answer. She hoped he wasn't upset. She could explain that it was her friends that had distracted her. Yet, that seemed almost like betraying her friends, as if they had become a hindrance in her life. The reality was that she would miss them, and terribly; and as much as she loved Jeff—and wanted to be with him on the island—

she knew she would grieve for all she was leaving behind.

She didn't want to grieve. She wanted love, she wanted Jeff, and she wanted her friends, too.

She guessed she wanted it all. Who didn't?

Her purse began to ring, and she felt her heart surge inside. It was Jeff! Who else would call this time of night?

"My purse! Where's my purse?" Katie reached over the seat, took it from her friend's hands, and pulled it into her lap. Digging frantically, she saw a flashing light and pulled it out, tapping the answer icon without looking, afraid he would hang up before she could tell him how sorry she was for not being there to catch his call.

She put the phone to her ear, and covering the mouthpiece with her other hand, she breathed, "Oh, I miss you so much. I love you more than anybody."

The reply was not quite what she expected.

"You do, Sweetie? Well, I love you, too. You know you're out of peanut butter, and oh, I'm taking your couch for the night. I used the embroidered cases, and thank you ahead of time. Oh, one last thing. Have you heard from Jeffie tonight?"

"From Jeff?" Katie heard the undertones in Winnie Catron's voice. This might be her best friend on the phone, but Winnie never asked anything innocently. If she wanted to know about Jeff, there was something going on.

Katie got distracted, though. Ashlynn had heard Jeff's name, and she grabbed the phone, calling into it,

"Jeff? Hi, Jeff! All our love!"

Katie never did get her phone back. It began the rounds, in spite of her protests. She did manage to convince the girls she had to get back to her car. A movie was simply not in store for a Monday evening, not with work the following morning.

And Winnie spending the night? Now what was that all about? With that phone call, it couldn't be good by anyone's measure.

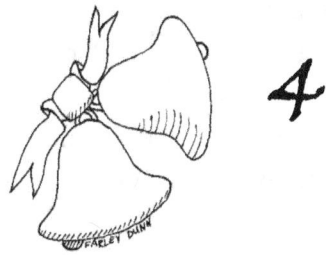

4

The overhead numbers in the elevator changed smoothly. In the background, Elvis sang about blue suede shoes, which meant it was after ten. Muzak commanded the airwaves between six and the bedtime hour. Oldies played until two, and the deep hours of the night were for the heavy metal freaks.

Katie's arms were filled with packages. Tissue paper overflowed one sack, and one crinkled red-and-gold bow she especially wanted to save kept falling to the floor. She couldn't leave any of it behind. She had to keep every piece to remind her of how much she had enjoyed the evening. She smiled when the King belted out "one for the money" a second time.

She leaned her head against the wall of the elevator and smiled. The trouble with money was that she didn't have any. Her grandmother once did, but Katie had been no more than a summer visitor on a craggy point running with an island pack of regulars. She had loved it every year, but she'd never considered how her grandmother paid for it all.

Now, the money was gone, her grandmother's house was gone, and she was heading back. She hoped for a lifetime spent on her favorite rock, one with Jeff Ragsdale, who had been her one-time childhood crush and would-be boyfriend.

It was all good, though. Who needed money when she would soon have Jeff forever and ever?

The car hushed to a stop, and with a gentle ding, one so well-mannered that Elvis paid no notice as he sang on about his wonderful shoes, the doors whooshed open, disappearing without any effort into the walls.

The hallway to Katie's apartment was tastefully appointed, if somewhat modern and stark. Directly in front of the elevator was a massive modernist painting, something with red and orange slashes partially covering a thick, black scribble, a vibrant, visual feast that she'd come to look forward to when arriving home. It was like a jolt of life, no matter how tiring the day had been.

She turned left, past two chrome and leather Breuer-designed Wassily chairs, wondering idly why no one ever sat in them. She'd been here for half-a-dozen years, and she'd never seen them used.

The hallway jogged past a dark-green slash of a window, one that hardly had a view of anything except a deep-set brick-and-stone cavern as it groped for a view of the city, but that was okay. The real windows were in the apartments, walls of them.

Then she was at her door, a post-modern slab made of layers of metal and wood, pierced by thick stained glass wedges that glowed with light from the other side. She frowned at that, as there should be no lights on in the apartment. Her friend Winnie knew better, as there was an electric bill to pay, and Katie had moving expenses to cover. That wasn't cheap.

When she went to unlock it, it slipped open easily, already unlatched.

"Winnie?" Katie pushed the door wide, irritated to see the overhead light blazing away full strength. She hit the switch and opened the alarm panel, cringing to see it wasn't set. Yet, nothing looked out of place, with not even the sofa pulled out for a bed, and she laughed softly in relief, calling out, "Shut the door next time, girl!"

Pushing the door to with her foot, she dropped her things onto a chair before stepping back to secure the apartment.

"Winnie?" Katie headed toward the bedroom. Her first evidence of her visitor's presence was on the bed, a jumble of vividly colored fabrics strewn across the foot. She groaned when she saw the bathroom door closed and light bleeding from underneath.

The floor began to vibrate, a sound Katie recognized, and she stepped to the bathroom door and rapped loudly. "Winnie! I hear you in there!"

The noise stopped, and after a moment the door opened. A shock of strawberry blonde hair appeared through the crack, and below it, a strikingly thin woman wrapped in a plush towel smiled at Katie.

"Hey, Sweetie. I didn't know how late you'd be, so I borrowed your tub. Do you need anything before I climb back in?"

She smiled disarmingly, but Katie pushed through, anyway. Yes, she did need in. Her toothbrush was alongside the sink, not in the hall bath. Without her toothbrush, she wasn't going to bed.

"See?" She held it up to Winnie before she walked back out the door. "Never come between a girl and her toothbrush. Oh, and I do have the loft, you know." As in, why did you tell me you were sleeping on the sofa? There's a bed up there.

"Oh, not tonight." Winnie pushed on Katie's shoulder to move her along with a giggle. "I can't let anyone see me like this. It just wouldn't do!"

The door shut in Katie's face, and she stepped back, confused. Who was there to see? The bathroom door made a noise, and Katie frowned, ready to bark at her friend when it began to open.

"Welcome home. I hope you enjoy your surprise!" Just a hand came through, it waved, and as it withdrew, the door closed with a click after it.

The floor began to vibrate again, and Katie knew she wouldn't get back in for at least an hour. Back in the living room, she pondered. It didn't make sense why Winnie had told her she was sleeping on the couch when it wasn't made up. Yet, there was Winnie's pillow in a chair, and neatly folded underneath, a set of sheets. She looked up, considering whether to sleep in the loft for the night and let Winnie have her bed. It was quite private, as long as she closed the French doors opening onto the living room; and there was a twin bed in the space, although the guest bath was on the main floor, and to hike down during the night for emergency visits wasn't very enjoyable.

Clearing her things away, the sound of running water from the hall bath got her attention. Tossing her belongings back onto the chair, she ran down the hallway to find the door closed, locked, and light shimmering from under the bottom edge. The shower was going full blast.

Winnie! How could she have turned the water on and then locked the door? It was a pair of men's shoes beside the door that suggested otherwise, and they caught Katie off guard. This wasn't like her friend at all.

Then Katie got angry. Bringing a man into her apartment? What was Winnie thinking?

The shower quieted, and Katie heard the curtain rumble back, the rings skittering on the metal rod. As angry as she was, she would be horrified to be caught eavesdropping. Once he was dressed, she would send him on his way, and then Winnie would hear what she thought about it. She headed to the bedroom to find out just who this was.

In that moment, the reality of the situation dawned on her. The alarm had been off. The door hadn't been latched correctly, and Winnie had already been in the bathroom. Did her friend even know a man was inside the apartment with her? She stepped to the bath door, ready to knock, when the blower kicked in on the tub. Katie dropped her hand. There was no way her friend would hear anything now.

9-1-1! Except . . . her phone was in her purse, and her purse was in there!

She jumped when she heard a cabinet door in the kitchen slam shut. Then the rattle of knives sliced into her awareness.

Her heart pounding, and tiptoeing carefully across the floor, Katie made sure the bedroom door was closed and locked. Breathing raggedly, she climbed on the bed and pulled the comforter up around herself. The front door . . . it had been open, and Winnie hadn't known. It frightened her that her friend might have been killed already, and it would have been Katie's fault, for living in Boston, for having this apartment, for not having a doorman to screen everyone who entered the building. He could have come in when another resident buzzed in a guest. Who knew? Dear God, she prayed, how will I ever forgive myself if another person I care about dies, and all because of me?

It was the television on the other side of the door that told her she might be stuck in here a very long time. The intruder was waiting on her to get home. He would probably wait all night. What would she and Winnie do?

She hugged the bedclothes tighter and hunkered down to wait. She had only one option: Pray and trust God to keep his hand on them, to keep her and Winnie safe from those that might harm them.

She was still frightened, though. God might help,

but that man was in her living room, and that wasn't reassuring in any way, form, or fashion.

What she really wanted was to cry.

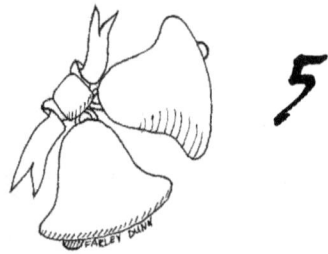

5

Katie jumped when she heard a door open. The remembered panic of the unknown intruder put him in the bedroom with her, even though she had securely locked the bedroom door.

It was Winnie that entered in a billowing cloud of steam, coming through the bathroom door with a white towel twisted around her hair, and wearing Katie's old pink bathrobe, the one Katie loved so very much.

Katie cringed when her friend headed directly toward the bedroom door.

"No, Winnie!" Katie tossed the covers aside and leaped from the bed, calling out in a strident whisper, "It's not safe!"

"Safe?" Winnie paused with her hand on the knob. "How can it not be safe?"

"There's a man out there. With knives." Katie still

had her pillow with her, and she hugged it. She moved beside the door, afraid that if they were heard, the intruder would force his way through. The sound of the television still came through the wall, so she was certain he hadn't gone anywhere. Things couldn't get more dangerous than this.

"Oh!" Winnie struggled to keep a smile from her face. "A man, and it's not safe. I see. It's not safe for you. For me? Sweetie, I adore men."

"No! Not this time," Katie hissed. "He even took a shower, like the whole apartment was his. There's no telling what he wants."

"You, apparently. It's your apartment." Winnie twisted the knob, only to find it locked, and she grunted in frustration when Katie grabbed her hand to keep her from unlocking it. "Swee-*tie!* Come on and let me though. I'm hungry."

"Me?" Katie's mind filled with fog, her thoughts closing in on what her friend had said to her. "What does he want with me?"

"Love, maybe." Winnie forced Katie's hand free, unlocked the door, and pulled it open. She leaned through, looking at Katie the entire time and calling out, "Jeffie! Katie-poo's crazy in love with you, with a strong emphasis on the crazy part. Come get her!"

"Winnie!" Katie whispered tersely, "You don't know who's out there."

"Sure," she laughed. "I let him in, silly goose! I'm your chaperone. This is your surprise." Winnie patted Katie's face and walked through to the other room, calling out, "What are you watching, Jeffie? *Love*

Boat?"

Mortification washed over Katie, and she felt her face burn. Jeff! How could she have thought . . . and she had hidden from him, not knowing he had driven to Boston . . . and it hit her. The missed phone call. Her extended evening with her friends. She wondered if he'd planned this all along, maybe had even been on the road when she'd talked to him that morning. That was so sweet if so, but it irritated her a bit, too. She would have been here, prepared for him if she'd known. She had a life, after all. She couldn't be expected to sit waiting on him, telling her coworkers, "Oh, Jeff might call. I have to sit by the phone."

And Winnie! That was mean, setting all this up, and then not telling her Jeff was here when she knew all along. Had she thought it was funny? Katie didn't.

Even so, Katie felt her eyes begin to burn. What was she thinking? Jeff, her Jeff had come to see her. Her Boston life might be unraveling as she stood here, with her pending resignation at ALDMass, the upcoming termination of her lease on this apartment, and even her friendships all going on hold for however long, but how many years had she dreamed of Jeff, her perfect Jeff riding up on a white horse to rescue her from a life of abandonment and loneliness? Well, maybe not on a white horse, but certainly piloting a white lobster boat. Then, just months ago, they had been reunited with her first trip back to the island in fourteen years, only to find he'd waited on her all that time.

And he was here! He was here!

"Katie?" It was Jeff's voice, deep and masculine. "Dame Carver, are you coming out? I did drive a long way, and all to see you. I've prepared a late supper, if you're hungry."

"One minute!" Good heavens, but she was an idiot! The knives. He'd been cooking! She couldn't let him see her crying! She darted for the bathroom door, closing and locking it firmly. The mirror was still fogged from her friend's extended bath, and Katie wadded a hand towel and wiped a spot clear. There her face was, surrounded by a halo of misty effervescence, her long, dark hair standing out in contrast against the cloudy mirror. Having Jeff here unexpectedly juxtaposed him vividly against her Boston life. To her, he was always her island man, handsome and rugged, and perfect in his island setting, whether digging for clams in the mud or sailing on the water with the residue of salt spray rimming his hair with white. Her Boston life was sidewalks and streetlights, with elevators, restaurants, and people who had only seen the ocean from the protection of double-glazed windows or driving I-90 on the way to Logan Airport.

The problem was that tonight, after being on the town with her friends, she knew what she was giving up.

She also knew what she was gaining—Jeff, her treasured memories of Rockhaven Island, and the life she'd always dreamed of—but what was being left behind tugged at her. Winnie, her best friend, always at her side. Connie, always calling her "dear" in a motherly way. Ashlynn and River, Kambri, Ellie and all the rest. They were her family, and she knew what would happen when she was gone. It had already happened with the island friends of her youth. They'd taken off in new directions, their lives diverged from hers, and rightly so. Yet, it meant they were no longer a family, and for the first fourteen years of her life, those island chums had been her family, as much as her grandmother and more than her parents ever could be. Why? Because they had loved something Katie had loved—and something her parents hadn't.

Her work friends loved their Boston life, even if some days they wished to sleep in or spend the day anywhere but at work; and although the ongoing slush of melting winter snows continually soaked their shoes, to live in Boston was to live at the center of the world. There was no better life than one lived in the finest city in America.

Katie knew what she was giving up. She was choosing to let go of something she loved, but that didn't make it easy. She hoped Jeff understood. He'd never loved city life, running back to spend his life on Rockhaven after his years in college. Katie was running back, too, but her reasons were different. She wasn't running from Boston. She was choosing something she loved better. Jeff would never grieve for the loss of all this. She would grieve for a very long time.

"Sweetie! Jeffie's waiting!" Winnie tapped three times very softly on the door. "The food's getting cold. Are you coming out anytime soon?"

"Just making sure I'm perfect. Be right there."

"Okay, Sweetie. I have some lemonade all made

up. I used all your lemons. So sorry! Come on out before Jeffie and I finish it all." She knocked another three times. "You are coming, please, Katie?"

"I'm there." Katie flushed the unused toilet. "Let me wash up."

"Um-kay. Don't take too long."

Katie took a deep breath in the silence, and she laughed. It was like an old song her dad used to listen to, something along the line of being torn between two lovers. Well, she didn't have either one, not as lovers, but she certainly had two loves. She was in love with Jeff, head over heels, and she wanted to spend every minute of her life with him. She had come to realize she was also in love with the life she had built for herself to stand in for the man she once thought she'd lost.

She was torn between two loves, and how was she ever to be happy with just one?

"Oh," she groaned aloud. Then, with determination in her backbone, the same determination she had sailed her skiff the Lil' Dude with during many an island gale, she grabbed the door knob and thrust herself through the door. Striding to the living room, she threw out her arms, and she let a smile spread across her face.

"Jeff, Winnie cannot have you one minute longer. Oh, I have missed you!"

It was when he swept her up in his arms and gave her a kiss that she knew she was making the right decision. She let herself melt into his embrace, certain that there was no choice at all. There never had been. Jeff, her island boy grown all rough and handsome, or her work friends, out for a night on the town? The only answer was Jeff, of course, and she'd known that all along.

Winnie had no problem inserting herself into the situation, though, laughing and calling out, "Break it up, you two. I'm still here."

Jeff chuckled, backing away, but Katie didn't let him get too far. Arm's length was about the right distance, where she could look into his eyes, and imagine never looking away again.

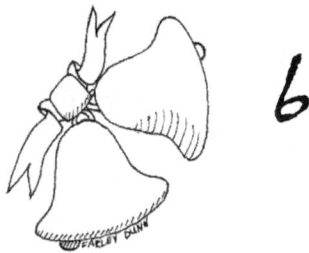

6

The Berkshires, Western Mass in all its mid-summertime glory, with flowers littering the shrubs like too-early Christmas bows, hinting at a distant but magical future coming quicker than anyone could imagine, spread the undulating landscape with vivid green.

The top was down on Jeff's Jeep, and the breeze was gentle as it whisked away the warmth of the afternoon sun. Katie waved her hand through the open window, letting it catch and dance in the onrush of air.

She smiled at Jeff in his wrap-around shades. He was tall enough that his hair caught and lifted in the breeze, giving him an engagingly boyish look. Out on the highway, the top had been securely up, but once they moved onto the back roads, Jeff had pulled to the shoulder and adroitly dropped the canvas covering, leaving their carriage for two open to the sky.

"We need sun," he'd laughed.

It was shade they mostly received, from the towering trees that crowded next to the road. Now Katie held his hand, and she enjoyed the warmth of his muscular grip.

"There." She pointed. It was a sign that directed them to their destination, an off-roading mecca, one with more muddy bogs for rampant wheel-spin than the green Jeep had ever seen in its life, or so Jeff had claimed.

"One day off, for me," Jeff had whispered in her ear the night before. "Surely they can give you one day."

"One day? That's all you want?" She'd laughed at that. He wanted her entire life. One day was only an appetizer, and not a very long one at that. "What could we do in one day here in Boston?"

What came to her mind was Fenway Park. Any man of any worth would be fascinated by the best sports facility in the Northeast. Or, a museum, maybe even the Museum of Fine Arts or the Gardner Museum. Then there was the Old North Church and the ship USS Constitution. And restaurants! LaGrassa's or Atlantic Fish. Her tummy rumbled just to think of it.

"Mud bogging." He'd grinned. "With you."

She'd pushed him away, shaking her head. He was teasing, right? Mud bogging?

"My Jeep. You know, I brought it with me, and Berkshire East is letting vehicles on a few lower trails."

"Berkshire East?" She'd looked across the room at Winnie. "Is that the one . . . ?"

"I think so, Sweetie. Two years ago with the church. Remember Roberto's broken wrist?" Winnie spooned a bite of ice from her lemonade into her mouth and began crunching away before turning back to the television.

"No self-respecting ski resort would let you bog on their trails. Seriously, now—"

"Seriously, now, yourself, Katie. They're rebuilding the trails, and this is a once-in-a-lifetime opportunity."

"You won't bog if it doesn't rain." Winnie wagged her spoon at him. "But we've already discussed that." She had her feet up under her, and she swung them to the floor, standing and heading for the kitchen.

"Before you got home," Jeff explained to Katie. "She's right, though. Mostly we'd be navigating the slopes, but I understand it's all dug up, so if it rains . . ." He smiled brightly.

"Thank John Deere for bulldozers." Winnie giggled from the kitchen.

"It's a long way." Katie saw the glossy images of Fenway and LaGrassa's fading away, to be replaced by towering trees, dusty jeans, and a very long ride back. She guessed it would be hot dogs and roadside hamburgers for their gourmet dining options, if they did this.

"Two hours, maybe three. If we leave by eight, we'll be there by lunch. Say yes. I've never had the Jeep on real trails before, and this might be my only chance until next summer."

"I will need to call my supervisor. Old Mass does still own me for several more weeks." Katie tried to shift gears quickly, sorting out in her head if she could do this with the presentation on Friday. "It's too late to call Connie tonight."

"Connie?" Jeff looked mystified.

"Her boss." Winnie was back in her chair, with a bowl of baby carrots in her lap. "And no, you don't."

Katie unwrapped Jeff's arms, and she stood, feeling, she had to admit, just a little perturbed. Her job was her responsibility, and she had done it well for half-a-dozen years. Just because she'd given notice didn't mean she could walk away from what she'd contracted to do when she hired on. "Winnie, what are you doing?" Her friend had pulled Katie's purse into her lap, and she proceeded to turn it over and dump it out.

"Just looking. Goodness, you keep everything in here, you know that? What would Calvin say if he saw what you did with his creation?"

"Calvin?"

"Klein, Sweetie. I should take you on a fashion shoot someday. You might learn something." After a moment she pulled Katie's phone from the disarray. She turned it on and unlocked it, tapping several times before holding it up for everyone to see. "Listen to this."

"Katie, dear, it's Connie. I just spoke with Lesly, and I'm so glad you girls had such a good time. It's after ten, and I think you need a day off. We'll see you on Wednesday, my gift to you. Tootles!"

"So we're all set?" Jeff had come up behind her, wrapping her in his arms. "My outdoor girl, in my outdoor world. What could be better than this?"

Well, it was Tuesday now, and the mountains were beautiful. They weren't Fenway, and the lobster roll they'd enjoyed hadn't quite been to LaGrassa's exacting standards, but she was full, and she'd enjoyed her lunch with Jeff.

What was wrong with her? Katie couldn't pin an exact tack into it, but she suspected her evening from the night before had something to do with it. No, not the evening with Jeff, but the one before that, with all her friends from work. It had been totally unexpected, had caught her completely off guard, and it had been exactly the sort of thing only the closest of coworkers would do for a good friend.

The part where the tack fit? Katie was shelving this part of her past voluntarily, choosing to close it up in a book, leaving the pages of her life high on a shelf to open from time to time, hoping to relive some of the best times she'd ever known in Boston. It was the same as on Rockhaven when she'd seen that picture of her and Jeff digging for clams that final summer before her grandmother's house burned to the ground.

The events of her childhood had been locked away in that photograph, and while it could be remembered, it could never be lived out again. It was tidily tucked away, to be pulled out for a rainy day, and while that was nice, it wasn't quite the same.

Ellie, Michelle, and the gang weren't rainy day

friends, and she didn't want to lose them.

She laid her hand on Jeff's arm, and when he turned to her, she smiled at him. She pointed to a second sign, this one leading into a grassy field. Off through the trees, glimpses of brown dirt lifted skyward. To the left they came to a sign attached to a tall pole, telling them if there was no attendant, to drop $50 into the attached lockbox and stay on the marked trails. The gates were locked at dusk.

That day, more than dust covered Katie's jeans before Jeff had his fill of off-road trekking. Four-wheel drive low was just the thing for maneuvering around newly cut tree stumps, snowless moguls, and Jeff's pride and glory, a mud pit.

Katie laughed harder than she ever thought possible. Only once was she attentive enough to be frightened when the off-road vehicle careened down a slope toward a patch of trees, but Jeff hooted, and throwing the gears into low, and gunning the engine, he left debris flying all the way to kingdom come.

One time during the day they saw someone else on the course, several teens in a lifted truck, bouncing crazily down the trails. Katie noticed a boy in back, holding to a roll bar, with his face lit up in excitement.

She knew just how he felt, except better. She had her best friend, excepting Winnie, of course, at her side. She and her fiancé were off for the day, just the two of them, doing something he loved—and that she was finding she thoroughly enjoyed, as well. Most of all, they were doing it together.

Afterward they found a family barbecue stand

along the side of the road, enjoying a plate together at an old picnic table under the trees. Now, with the top still down, and the wind whipping Katie's hair, she held Jeff's hand with one, and toyed with the air with the other.

She had a wedding on her mind, one that wasn't that far away. Watching the Christmas-ribbon bushes flash by in their bright sparks of summer color, she imagined how it might be, Christmas on the island. She'd never done that, been there for the holidays.

That was in the future, and Jeff was in her present. She pulled the hair from her face with her right hand, and she turned to him, catching his profile against the late afternoon sky. He was everything she'd ever imagined him to be, and they might not have dined at LaGrassa's, but they'd dined together, and for that, she'd ride the slopes with her man any day of the week.

She smiled at that, turning back to look through the dirt-splattered windshield. She'd rather ride the waves in her sailing boat, but whatever was fine with her, as long as Jeff was at her side.

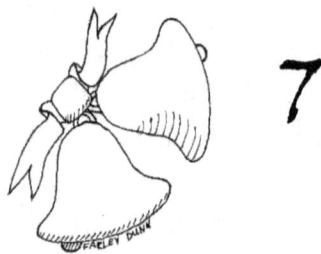

7

"For one hundred sixty-five, that's right." Katie turned the florist's brochure over, pointing to one picture, although it couldn't be seen over the phone. "Baby's breath, can you do that, too? White mixed with baby blue, maybe a fifty-fifty mix?"

Part of the difficulty in planning her upcoming wedding was the fifteen miles of ocean between the shore and the island. There were ferry schedules to coordinate, caterers to organize, and decisions to make on where to bed down those from off island!

"Yes, there is," she responded to the phone. "Dyer's Delivery can pick up from the mainland. Will the flowers need refrigeration? This is an island we're talking about, and I'll need time to set things up."

Another twenty minutes and an explanation that Styrofoam refrigerator packs would do quite nicely to preserve the exquisite beauty of Katie's preferred blooms had her almost rolling her eyes. Still, if she was paying for them, she wanted everything to be perfectly beautiful on her wedding day.

The flowers had been the easy part, though, she was finding out. The cake? Corrine's Creations, an on-island bake shop, had seemed to fit the bill nicely, until Katie learned they mostly did cookies and cupcakes for birthdays and school functions. This was their first wedding ever, and they had never done a wedding cake. However, over the phone the mother and daughter team had been so enthusiastic that Katie hadn't had the heart to break theirs. Besides, she accepted with resignation, she would soon be living with these people. She had already contacted them, and she couldn't back out gracefully, not with the wedding being a major island event.

Later, Jeff told her the two women attended his church regularly, and Katie was horrified that she might have driven a wedge into her life on the island even before setting a permanent foot on its shores. For days afterward she wondered what other mine fields she would have to maneuver within island politics to keep her future life glued together properly.

The clock on her desk spoke of her lunch hour slipping quickly away, and as she pulled out her microwavable soup from her desk drawer, the phone rang.

"Katie Carver. How may I help you?" Even during lunch, she wouldn't refuse to answer her line. All incoming calls routed through the switchboard, and if it came through on her time, it was personal. Suzie on the switchboard was good about that.

"Katie? Is this little Katie, from Boston Katie? Oui?"

"Yes, this is Katie from Boston. Who am I speaking with?" *Little* Katie? She hadn't been called little Katie in twenty years!

"I am so pleased to make this contact with you once again. I hear this most happy news, and I will be soon arriving at your JFK Airport. I would be making reservations for my stay at a very good location. You may have a suggestion, s'il vous plait?"

"You need a hotel room." Katie stated it as a fact. What else could her caller mean? The "happy news" could only be her upcoming wedding. But her JFK? She didn't live anywhere near JFK. That was New York.

"Oui."

The speaker at the other end of the phone was so animated and pleased-sounding that Katie hated to suggest she might be coming in to the wrong airport, but Boston would be a better choice. She still didn't have a name, although Katie had an idea how to draw it out of her caller.

"What name should I register you under?"

"Ah, your grandmamma always say I am so empty-headed. You do not remember me from so many years before. I am Nicolette, my little Katie. You remember, now? From your party, when you were cinq, non, five year of age. You must be remembering Cousin Nikki, non?"

"Nikki!" Nikki? The name seemed . . . somewhat familiar. Then she pictured an elegant woman with a fur collar on every item of clothing she wore, even her swimsuit. The party. The party! Yes, she had been five, and her parents had come to the island. It was the Fourth, and the grounds had been crowded with people. Katie remembered wanting them all to go away.

"You remember Nikki! Oui?"

"The Fourth of July, right?"

"Ah, I knew you could not forget. I gave you a little ring, one with a very small stone. You have it still, oui?"

"Oh, I do remember." And Katie did. She had left the ring on the windowsill that last day on the island, knowing it would be in the same location when she returned in the spring. "You do know my grandmother's house was destroyed in a fire when I was fourteen. Nothing was saved."

"Ah, ma chère! How could I be so silly! Of course, of course. You have nothing but your grandmamma's love remaining. I am so old a fool. Now, to business. I need rooms, and for quite some time. I have not been to America in many years, and to fly, well, is not so good on me anymore. I will take this chance to enjoy your country's fine hospitality for the extended period. You will help me, ma chère?"

"That will be wonderful. I'll set things up. If I can get a return number?" Katie's clock was winding lunch down, and her soup sat, unopened and unheated. She sighed, but she would live. She wrote down Cousin Nikki's information, promising to get back with her soon, making sure she got the dates of her flight.

It was after she hung up that she kicked herself. With the flower worries, the cake, and then the surprise of a second cousin she hadn't seen in over twenty years, she forgot all about JFK. Nikki needed to fly into Logan. Perhaps her flight could still be changed. She reached for the phone to call her back when it began to ring.

Katie glanced at the clock. Lunch was over, and that meant this was work-related. Suzie was good, and that meant Suzie was with the clock. Anything personal now would jump directly to voicemail.

"Katie Carver, Old Mass Claims Department. How may I assist you?"

"I need a repair."

"Ah, yes. We will get you back on the road in a jiffy. As we say here at Old Mass, you only have to call us once. Have you already had your car looked at by a claims specialist?"

"Sweetie, it's not my car that needs repaired." The caller giggled.

"Winnie?"

"Of course, silly goose." Winnie giggled again.

"I'm working. You can't call me now." Katie put her hand over the button to cancel the call as soon as she made herself clear. She was not allowed personal calls during business hours.

"Oh, that's why I have a repair. Otherwise, I get that machine, and I can't talk to you then. Now, I've been thinking about those bridesmaids atrocities you plan for us to wear, and I have a better idea. There's someone I know—"

"No, Winnie. I'm not going there. Enough is going wrong as it is. Now I've got my cousin coming in, and I've got to find her a place to stay."

"Your cousin? Now that's a horse of a different color. What cousin?" It sounded like Winnie was chewing gum and popped a bubble too near the phone. "Maybe she could help plan the new dresses. Or is it a he?"

"She." Winnie sounded more hopeful than Katie thought she should, and she decided she'd better set her straight. "She's from France, she's really old, and she's flying into JFK."

"New York? That's hours away!"

"Are you offering to pick her up?" Hope lit up Katie's mood.

"Sweetie, I don't have the time. Remember, I've got this dress mess to untangle. I will not wear an atrocity for anyone, not if other people can see me. Sorry, not even for you."

"Ooh, Winnie! Why do I keep you for a friend, anyway?" One more thing going wrong, and Katie felt she would shatter, and she still hadn't had lunch. She wanted to snap someone's head off. Winnie had better be glad she was on the other end of the line, and not here in person.

"Because I love you. So I can go now. Thanks for letting me redo all the dresses. I've got everything under control." The line clicked, and she was gone.

"Winnie?" Katie tapped the line, but all she got was the dial tone. She dropped the receiver heavily into its cradle. She had not given her friend permission to redo all the dresses, had not even hinted at it.

The phone rang again, and Katie grabbed it, prepared to bark at Winnie for assuming entirely too much. When she pressed the button, her remarks were preempted by her supervisor.

"Katie? This is Connie. We've got a situation. I need you here in my office, dear, ASAP."

"Certainly. I'll be right there."

Katie placed the phone down gently, and looked longingly at her uneaten cup of soup. What fun they could have had together. Oh, well. Soup, soup, come again another day. She opened her desk drawer and dropped it inside; and pushing it shut, she grabbed her pen and tablet and stepped from her desk.

Before she headed outside, she double checked the cabinet securing her purse. Satisfied, she flipped off the lights and walked away, leaving her office silent and in the dark.

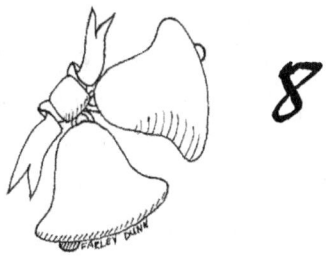

8

"Hey, Kam. Free for lunch today?"

It was Saturday, and the meetings at work the day before had run long. Katie had worn out long before the sessions had ground to a close. Being presenter at many of them hadn't helped. She needed out and about; a change of scenery.

A nice lunch might help, she had decided. And company. She desperately needed company. A good friend, someone just to sit with and talk about nothing at all. Kambri was her Saturday regular, mostly in the depths of winter, but Katie wouldn't be here this winter, would she?

Katie had her phone in front of her, watching the screen in speakerphone mode, her friend's picture smiling back at her.

"I'm watching my nephew, today, so it might be a

MacDonald's run. How 'bout that, Harry? You want to go to Micky-D's and play in the bounce room?" She could be heard calling to someone Katie couldn't see.

"Kambri, don't tease. He'll expect to actually find one."

"Nah, he's three. Kids retain one minute for every birthday they've had. So, in three minutes he's rebooted and ready for something new. If more parents realized that, they'd do a lot better job parenting." In the background, it sounded like the boy threw something that banged against a glass object. "No, no, Harry. Micky-D's. There we go, give Auntie Kammie the shoe. Thank you. Want to go see Auntie Katie?"

"Yah! Auntie Kay-Kay!" He screamed so loud Katie heard him just fine.

"On Massachusetts? Will that do?" Katie had cringed at the sound of the three-year-old's excitement, but she needed company. A super-charged three-year-old explosion on steroids might not be her first choice, but still, today she'd take what she could get.

Before she hung up, she had instructions to pick up her friend and to bring along a cookie, if she had any. Harry's visit had been a surprise to Kambri, and the boy was ravenous. Sugar or peanut butter? Katie had asked. Anything the child could eat, Kambri had replied.

"Oh, no," Kambri moaned when they drove around the block towards the restaurant. "You would come here. We'll never get the kid away."

It was the Boston Fire Department, their Arson Squad.

"All little boys love fire trucks." Katie put on her blinker, her little Beetle slowing to a stop as she waited for three cars to pass. The sun was in her eyes, and she lowered her shade just as an open spot appeared. Pulling through the gap in the busy Saturday traffic, she slipped smoothly into the lot.

"Yeah, and they scream when you drive away." Kambri turned to the back, and reaching over the seat, she pulled the remains of a cookie out of the boy's hand. "No more for you until after you eat."

"We see fire trucks?" He pointed out the window where the front of one, bright red, could just be seen.

"Sure, Harry. See? Now you've seen a fire truck." She glanced at Katie and shrugged. "You do what you gotta do. Let's get the little guy inside and some fries inside him."

"You know, we could walk over and look at one." Katie whispered as she opened her door, leaning Kambri's direction. "They've got several parked outside."

The building next door to the restaurant was huge, and Katie was pretty certain the Boston Fire Department loved kids. Who knew but what one might grow up and join the ranks. Anyway, she'd done an insurance claim for a captain at this location. If he were here, she was pretty certain he'd be glad to talk to the boy.

Kambri just laughed and took off after her nephew, catching him by the collar when he almost ran in front of a car backing out of a space.

Inside, with Harry's child-oriented meal keeping him occupied, and the women's more adult fare spread

55

before them, they finally had a chance to talk.

"So," Kambri began, "what about this?" She motioned with her forkful of salad at the building around them. "You have this? On the island?"

Katie laughed, and then she apologized. "You don't know Rockhaven."

"Okay, then tell me." She dug into her salad and hefted another load of greenery. "How do you keep kiddos happy without one of these?"

"We put them in boats and let them drift in the tide."

"Get out, girl! No way!" Kambri waved her hand dismissively.

"Get out, girl!" Harry repeated, smearing a fry into his catsup and sucking the condiment off before repeating the action.

Katie laughed. "Would you like half of this?" She had a sandwich, but she'd cut it in two and didn't think she'd be able to eat it all.

"Me? Just my salad. Thanks."

"I'm going to miss all of you more than I expected." Katie hadn't planned to say that, but it was true. "Monday was so much fun."

"Nah! You'll have a man, and you'll forget all about us, and you're welcome about Monday. It was mostly Connie, though." Kambri reached out and patted Katie's arm once.

"Have a man," Harry intoned, picking up on his aunt's words, before sucking another dollop of catsup from his increasingly soggy fry. He smacked his lips and said, "Forget about it."

"Harry's cute." Katie smiled, pointing. "Forget about it. He's not paying us any mind, and still, he hears every word."

"And repeats every single one to my sister. I have no secrets when the little nephew's around." Kambri laughed, sucking a smear of dressing off one finger. "I found that out when he was two, and my sis knew every detail of a phone call I made. He's got tape-recorder memory, my dad says. With no erase mode."

"Any juicy details to embarrass you?"

"Listen. Harry?" She reached over and tapped his table.

"What?" He was sucking the French fry all the way in, and he began to chew.

"Hi, Rosa . . ."

"Did you run the 'thon this year?" He was on a fresh fry, and it looked like he wasn't listening at all.

"Watch this," Kambri whispered, pointing. Louder, she said, "At the gym . . ."

"I met a cute guy." Harry sucked, and red catsup disappeared. He went on, sticking the fry back into his catsup, and mumbling on about something else.

"You poor girl." Katie shook her head. It was amazing, though.

"Just be careful what you say. At odd moments, something'll trigger his memory, and he'll say whatever he's heard, no matter what it was." Kambri was finished by then, and she set her plastic bowl on the tray, pushing the whole thing to the side. "Now tell me, what did you do with your honey the other day? We all know that's where you were on Tuesday."

"I should have known I couldn't keep it secret. You had to have learned that from Winnie."

"Of course. We're friends, and I get all her Facebook posts. You and Jeff were so cute there on your sofa. Now, Tuesday. You don't post, so I never know unless I ask. Where'd you eat? Please say Island Creek. That's the yummiest place in the city."

"Not exactly. Try roadside barbecue." At Kambri's look of dismay, Katie explained. "He brought his Jeep up, and we took it to the Berkshires mud bogging."

"No! Mud bogging?" Kambri began to laugh. "Are you sure you found the right man? I can't imagine you in a mud bog, ever. Did Jeff get in, too?"

"We both did."

"I bet Jeff had fun." Kambri winked.

"Bet Jeff had fun," Harry repeated, now on his third fry.

Katie rolled her eyes, the wink explaining a lot. "Not mud wrestling, Kam. Mud bogging. We were in the Jeep driving through the mud, perfectly clean and dry." Well, not exactly clean and dry, but certainly not rolling around in it. What was her friend thinking?

"I like my version better. Oh, well." Kambri sucked on her straw, only to have it gurgle with air. She set the paper cup beside her salad bowl and put her elbows on the table, resting her chin on her hands, and watched Harry smearing red up and down the side of his drink cup.

Marching music broke the moment of silence.

"That's me!" Kambri pulled her purse up and dug out her phone, laying it flat on the table. Tracing a design on the face, she tapped an icon, and two seconds later, she spoke to it. "Hey, Sis. What's going on?"

"Jeb and I finished lunch, and now we find the movie's sold out. You want we should come get Harry?" The voice was gritty over the speaker phone, but it was loud enough to get Harry's attention.

"Mommy?" He was licking his fingers, and he looked up.

"Hi, Baby. Want Mommy and Daddy to come pick you up?"

"Get out, girl!" He laughed, reaching for the phone.

"Kambri, what's that about?"

"We're with a friend out by the fire hall, the one for arson. He overheard us talking."

"Off Mass Ave?"

"Sure, I think so." Kambri glanced at Katie, waiting until she nodded. "Yeah, that's the one."

"We're not too far. We'll be there in ten minutes. Sit tight."

"Kay. See ya." Kambri tapped the phone to turn it off. She smiled at Katie. "That was easy."

"That was easy." The boy was down to licking the side of his drink cup, and he had catsup smeared across one side of his face.

"Your sister's sweet. Should you clean Harry up before she gets here?"

"Probably." Kambri stood and held out her hand for his. "Let's go potty with Auntie Kammie. It'll be fun." She looked at Katie, made a face, and shook her head before laughing. The boy grabbed her hand with

59

his catsup-covered one, and they headed off down the aisle.

Katie looked out the window at the traffic passing by. A car very much like Jeff's, except red, pulled in the service station across the road, and two young women got out, both wearing denim shorts and tee shirts, looking like they were headed out to enjoy a summer day that was quickly approaching hot. From the main dining room, she couldn't see the fire department, but that was just as well. Her friend was apparently right, because three minutes after stepping inside, Harry had forgotten all about the fire trucks, and he'd become engrossed in his catsup. Perfect, since his parents were on the way.

Mud bogging. She'd had a good time with Jeff. There was no doubt in her mind about that. Without him? Tuesday's activities wouldn't have been on her radar. It was Jeff she'd enjoyed.

She missed him. Immensely.

He should be with her here. Today. At this family-oriented, child-friendly restaurant. Then they could tour the fire trucks together, and they'd be building memories here in Boston.

She wondered if that was part of the dark mood she seemed to be under. She loved Jeff; more than anything she loved him. She needed him mixed up in her Boston life. The Berkshires? That had been nice. Rockhaven? Even nicer. However, her Boston life was separate, all her own, and while she loved Jeff, she loved Boston, too, the traffic, the restaurants, even the big red fire trucks that tooted their horns when navigating the crowded streets.

Her friends? They'd meet Jeff for one fun weekend, and they'd never really know him, except Winnie. And she'd only met him in July, and then, of course, letting him into her apartment and serving as a good chaperone for the night.

Come back, Jeff, she called mentally. Come and get me, my love. I need you to be part of all this, so I can turn it loose when it's time.

He didn't hear her, though. He was a day's drive away, probably on the island, out of range of her phone.

She made up her mind. She was phoning him today, once she dropped Kambri off. If the call didn't go through, she would try and try until it did. She needed the sound of his voice to keep her on track. She had two worlds, both tugging at her heart. She knew which one would eventually claim her, but it would be easier with Jeff's voice in her ear.

She looked back into the restaurant to see Kambri and Harry heading her direction. Kambri had her face twisted in a frown, and Harry was dragging hard behind her.

"Is everything all right?" Katie moved the boy's things off his table to where he couldn't reach them.

"It will be when my sister gets here." Kambri smiled brightly.

Katie knew that look, and she fought a smile. She'd seen it on her friend Janine Roscoe Peavey's face out on Rockhaven, but in reality, there was no comparison. Kambri had been penned up with one boy for five minutes in the restroom. Janine was penned up on an island in the freezing weather with four boys all winter every winter.

Even so, Katie felt better, somehow, like she'd made a connection between her Boston life and her island home. In that moment, she was certain Jeff was the right choice, and she relaxed.

In fact, there was no doubt in her mind. She'd known it all along.

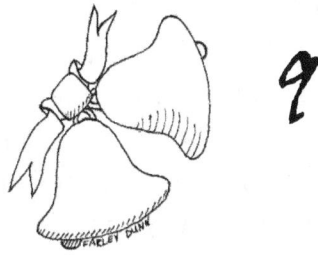

9

"**R**ain." Katie stood at the window holding her phone in her hand, and she could hear it ringing on the other end. Drops of water splattered against the glass, melting into the moisture already coating the slick surface, and giving the scene outside a distorted, otherworldly appearance.

It didn't brighten her mood much. She was meeting Winnie for breakfast before morning services, and she was having trouble getting moving. She was dressed, though, and ready to go, if only after much moaning and complaining.

"Winnie, here." The voice on the phone's speaker sounded out of breath, as if she had been running up a flight of stairs.

"Hey, Honey!" Katie brightened her tone, in spite of the gray world outside. "Are we still on for breakfast?"

"Let me see." Winnie's voice grew faint. "It's 8:40 now, and services start at 9:00. My hair, and nails . . ." She grew louder, even more out of breath. "Oh, oh, there's no way I can make the next service. I'm so sorry, Sweetie. I forgot to plug in my rollers. How about 10:40, Wendy's or Burger King?"

"Sure, either." The choice of restaurants didn't matter. Both were right across the street from Trinity, Winnie's current church of the moment. "Why so late? I'm hungry now." What she meant was that they might be attending the 11:15 service, but they could meet for breakfast anytime.

"Sweetie, I have to be beautiful, and it has to be the real thing, not just crawl-out-of-bed beautiful. Now, my treadmill's saying I'm burning calories, and I'm not even on it, so, see you on the way!"

The line clicked off, and Katie set her phone aside. Immediately she picked it back up, finding her recent calls list, and pulling up Jeff's name. She wanted to phone him now, but he would be in services of his own by this time, and she couldn't interrupt simply because it was raining outside.

Last night's call hadn't been all she'd hoped it would be. She'd gotten through, but Jeff had been in his car—an Al and Janine emergency—and the call had cut out twice. She'd returned it once, concerned that one of her old friend's four rowdy boys might be ill or injured, and the second time? He'd been nearly to Janine's, telling Katie Al had called, and he didn't really know what it was about. When that call dropped, too, she'd let it go. He'd sounded horrendously busy, anyway, and she supposed his parishioners needed him pretty badly.

Her husband, a preacher. Did she know what she was getting herself into?

Tapping the face of her phone, Katie knew she could not remain in this apartment. Heading out, she pulled an umbrella from the entry console and made sure this time the door was firmly shut and the alarm engaged. Someone called to her from down the hall.

"Miss Carver!" The voice was cracked, and it wavered in an ancient soprano. "Are you headed to early services?"

Katie turned to see a petite woman, maybe five feet if she tiptoed, with white hair swirled around her head. Anabelle Rosenbaum, although Katie had heard her friends call her Annie. She sprouted an off-center pillbox hat enveloped in rose-embroidered netting. She was really quite an adorable sight coming down the hall, the perfectly coifed little old lady in this ultramodern building.

"If I can make it on time. It's Anabelle, isn't it?" She hadn't thought about attending the earlier service alone, just intended to get out, but she might at that.

"Annie, if you please. Or, as my old auntie used to say, s'il vous plait." She smiled, her bright-red lipstick cutting a pleasant slash across her face. "She was French, you understand, old money and all that. She gave me this hat, you must know, in the forties; brought it from France. Vichy. There was a war on."

"World War II." They were at the elevator by then,

and Katie tapped the down button. "Germany."

"Don't forget Japan, my dear, but that was the other side of the world." Anabelle tapped her chest just at the throat with the fingers of one hand. "Ah, I should not confuse the two. Japan was very different. They wanted manufacturing materials. Germany wanted to kill the Jews. I am Jewish, you know."

"I didn't know that." Katie tapped the lobby button, and the doors closed them in. "Are you headed to the synagogue?"

"Not practicing, dear. Just Jewish. It's a race, not only a religion. Dear, I am converted, a good Christian, as are many of my fellow race. I do believe I attend at your fellowship." Her voice brightened when she said that.

"Trinity?" Katie never would have dreamed. Boston was so large, and Trinity was just one church out of the many throughout the city. "You're attending the 9:00 service?"

"Every Sunday, my dear. I've seen you there once or twice, with your friend." She motioned with her hands in a circle around her head. "The pretty one? With the hair?"

"Winnie." Katie smiled. "She travels for work, but when she's here, we attend together."

"Not that you're not pretty, my dear. You are, and very young. I've seen your friend. Macy's. Only the prettiest girls model for Macy's. I get their ads, you see, and I look at them. I like nice things."

The elevator sounded, and the doors opened into the lobby. Katie smiled, and she held her hand out to

Anabelle.

"S'il vous plait."

"Oh, oh, my dear," and Mrs. Rosenbaum tittered. "No need to speak French to me. I'm not French at all." She tittered again, and it was obvious she enjoyed hearing Katie say the words.

"Then, if you please." Katie motioned and followed her new friend into the tall, spare, and neatly organized foyer. "You do speak French, though. You sounded so fluent earlier."

"Oui." Mrs. Rosenbaum tittered. "Oh, my dear, I haven't said that in decades. You, dear? Are you French?"

"Hardly." Katie laughed. At the door, she glanced at Annie. "Your umbrella?"

"No, no, dear. I don't carry one. My driver, he will have one for me." Annie smiled, stepping through the door to stand under the overhang. "He should be here any minute."

Katie smiled. Driver? Anabelle wore a hat that was counting down to a century old, and she had a driver?

When the van pulled up at the curb, Katie understood. On the side it said Senior Transport, LLC. A tall man in a uniform exited the driver's door with a black umbrella in his hand. When he got to Anabelle, he opened it and held it waiting.

"We have to hurry if we're making the 9:00, Miss Annie. Stand next to me. We can't have you getting your hair wet." He smiled at her, as if he knew her pretty well.

"Carl, this is my friend, and she is attending with

67

me this morning. May she ride along?" Anabelle patted Katie gently on the arm, smiling brightly at Carl.

"Well," Carl started, hesitating. "You are my only passenger, so I guess it's okay. Afterwards, though, I can't promise. If I'm full—" He let it go at that.

"I appreciate it, Carl." Katie was quick to express her gratitude, although she would have been glad to walk or catch the subway. This was about Anabelle, though. With an invitation like this, it would be rude not to accept it wholeheartedly. "If you're full afterward, I can find my way to the T with no trouble."

"Yes, ma'am," he said, nodding his head. "You understand how it is. If I'm empty, and a qualified rider wants to take a guest, I can sometimes accommodate them, but if I'm full or almost full, then I have to allow for those who qualify." He'd said the word twice, telling Katie he was reiterating company policy, not his own. "Sundays aren't usually full, so if you want a ride back, as long as Miss Annie's with you, well, I'll be glad to have you along." He shrugged and smiled.

At the van, a step extended beneath the opened door, enabling Anabelle to enter slowly but carefully, and once she was aboard, Katie climbed in after her. Carl pulled out smoothly, navigating the nearly empty streets, and in only minutes, they were at Trinity Church. He reversed his procedure, stopping out front, providing the protection of his black umbrella, and walking Anabelle to the door.

He thanked Katie for her understanding, and closing his umbrella, he stepped back into the rain, flashed his brake lights, and pulled smartly away from the curb.

Katie didn't normally attend this particular service, and now she wondered why. It was the family service, with peppy music and active participation by the youth and the choir.

The service was just starting as they entered, and Anabelle seemed to know everyone, stopping to shake hands and to pat small children on the head. She went so far as to introduce Katie to several people, most in Annie's age bracket, but several younger.

They sat four rows from the front, under the massively domed ceiling. With the rain outside, the light from the gigantic stained glass windows was softened, and the whole place had a charmed, fairy tale feel.

This close to the front, Katie was reminded of a summertime service not so long ago when she had sat at the front of a similar service, honored as a special guest, and even found the man she wanted to live with for the rest of her life. Winnie had been there with her that Sunday, but this wasn't too bad. She had Annie with her as a stand-in, and with her little gauze-infused pillbox hat with its rose embroidery, who could say but this wasn't as fine a friend as anyone had ever had.

The minister was somewhat different, though. That summer Sunday, her minister had been tall and handsome, with slab-sided cheeks that broke into the most endearing dimples. His fly-away hair had hardly been tamed, even in his ecumenical robes, and when she'd run in frustration from his wonderfully supportive congregation, he'd chased after her, leaving his church leaderless and confused.

What would this minister do if she ran out the door in the middle of his service, only to stand on the steps with tears running down her face? Would he come running after her?

Well, actually, she hoped not. She would be mortified; but she didn't intend to run from this man at any point. Rather, it seemed she would be sitting through his ministry two times this morning. After all, she was here now, she would be having brunch with Winnie afterwards, and she would return for yet another service after that.

This had better be good, she thought. Her stomach was rumbling, and she was missing Jeff about as much as she could miss anyone.

She was also irritated at Janine. She'd really wanted to have Jeff to herself for a little while the night before, and those four wild ones she was raising had taken her place.

It was partly the hunger, Katie knew, but she envied the members of Rockhaven Town Church. They had Jeff Ragsdale, and she didn't.

Miss Annie must have seen the longing on her face, because she patted Katie's arm and whispered, rather too loudly, "It's okay, my dear. I was lonely when I didn't have a man, too. God will bring one your way. Just you wait and see."

Several people looked Katie's way, and she thought about running at that point, but Jeff would not be at the door to catch her, and what would she do for an hour and a half? Then, she began to chuckle. It was funny, in a way. God had already brought her a man, just that he was in Maine, and she was here. Did God see the irony in that, or was Katie the only one that understood? Her in Boston and Jeff in Maine? What good did that do?

The congregation stood to begin a choral reading, and Katie had to put her self-commiseration aside. It was Sunday, and Sunday was for God, worship, and finding peace in Him. She would eventually find her peace, even if she had to wait until she was in Maine to do so.

She joined in, "The Lord is my Shepherd, I shall not want . . ."

In her mind, though, she imagined a good breakfast sandwich from Burger King, or even Wendy's. She didn't care. She was hungry, and all the psalms in the Bible couldn't feed that.

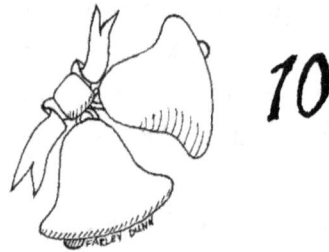

10

Katie sat across a dining booth from Winnie, and she chuckled. She had exchanged one brand new friend, for one very old friend. The thought made her smile, as her new friend was very old, and her old friend sported a very new hairstyle. Well, it was as new as a new color could make it.

"You will be back for the wedding?" This was important to Katie. Winnie had done shoots in Dallas, Atlanta, and L.A.; and once in Calgary. That one had been in the middle of winter, and she'd vowed never again, no matter that it had paid better than any other job, before or since.

This shoot was in the Bahamas, for Disney. She would soon be famous, Winnie had giggled over her paper cup of diet soda.

"Sweetie, I'll be back for next weekend. You have

a shower on Friday, remember. I plan to be there." She waggled a finger, with a twinkle in one eye. "Might be getting you something pretty special, if you know what I mean."

"So, back to you. When do you leave?" For the photo shoot, Katie knew her friend understood.

Winnie sighed and rolled her eyes. "In the morning. Who knew planes actually flew at 6:30?" She brightened. "The good thing is I'll be there by noon. More time in the sun is what I say."

"That's the reason for the hair?" It was pulled back to the nape of her friend's neck, tied with a scarf, and woven into a thick braid below that. It was also bright red.

"You know Disney! There's not a strawberry bone in their body. So, I'm red for the week." She smiled brightly and took a bite of her breakfast sandwich. She wrapped the food securely in its packaging before setting it back down, patting it gently. "Stay warm little sandwich, in case I need another bite."

"On a diet? Are they getting you into a swimsuit for the week?"

"If they want, but I think I might be a beach hostess. They're shooting a new brochure. This face is going worldwide. And you knew me before I was famous. Lucky you. Touch me while no one knows me. Say you were the first." She held out her hand to Katie.

"No thanks. You just make sure you get on that plane back home, and make sure you get here on time. The shower's at four."

"Yes, ma'am." She held her hand out to the family sitting at the next table, calling to them, "I'm going to be famous. Touch me while you still can." They looked at her strangely and moved to the other side of the room.

"See? They have the right idea." Katie teased, but she had an eye on the clock, also. It was nearly eleven. "Ready? Second service starts in a few minutes."

"Third." Winnie slurped from her cup, and she dropped it and her unfinished sandwich into the bin behind her. "I missed the second, remember?"

"I didn't. This is my second service. This morning."

"Seriously?" Winnie grabbed Katie's arm and looked her hard in the face. "Are you getting all religious on me? I thought I was the good one."

"Yes, Miss Bikini Queen. I'm getting all religious on you. For your information, I made a new friend this morning, and we went to the 9:00 service together." She peeled her friend's fingers from her arm.

"Oh?" Winnie finally looked interested. "Can I get a name?" She patted her lips with her paper napkin and dropped it in the waste bin, also.

"Anabelle." Let Winnie stew on that. "She has a car and a driver and everything, and she speaks French." Katie grinned wickedly.

"Oh, French! I love French." Winnie grabbed Katie's arm and squealed. "Introduce us. Promise you will! I can practice! Au contraire . . . bon appétit . . . oh là là! Oh, I can say something else. Let me see . . . je t'aime. That means—"

"I love you. I know. Maybe at the shower, if she can come." Katie hadn't yet invited her, but who knew? "Now, though, want to share my umbrella?"

The rain had become a torrent while they were eating, and the sidewalk in front of the restaurant glistened, with bright spatters skipping up every few inches, like little hands reaching for the sky. It would be an impossible dance to avoid every one. Still, Katie figured, if they ran, what with the umbrella, they might just keep their hair relatively dry.

"Ready, Honey? Wet feet and all, but oh, well!" Katie smiled brightly, remembering childhood summers running barefoot in the rain on Rockhaven.

"Almost," Winnie said. She reached down and pulled her shoes off. "Versace. I'll carry mine."

"You silly girl! Barefoot in Boston!" Katie laughed, wondering if she dared. Hose might be twenty bucks, but her shoes were five times that.

"I've got a bag." Winnie pulled a thin plastic sleeve from an invisible pocket, and she dropped hers inside. "I'll carry yours, too."

The rain continued to increase, and Katie kicked hers free, dropping them in her friend's bag. Laughing, they hugged each other tightly, the umbrella stretched over them both, and headed into the torrent.

At the curb, the flood gurgled along nearly six inches deep. By then they no longer cared. Their stockings were soaked, and while they might survive to be worn again, they couldn't get any wetter. Winnie let out a high-pitched wail when they hit the first curb, and Katie joined her by the time they got to the second. Reaching the church vestibule, they realized they couldn't put their shoes back on, not without letting their feet dry, so they smiled guiltily and shrugged when the greeters glanced at their dripping hose; and leaving Katie's umbrella behind, they tiptoed into the sanctuary, finding the first empty seats to remain as close to the back as possible.

Clearly this was a time for worshipping the Lord, but the storm outside had them laughing harder than they had laughed in a very long time, and Katie couldn't help but think God would approve. They were across the building from where they usually sat, and the faces they recognized filed in from the farthest doors. Several couples greeted them, and a family with a trio of preteen girls trailed in. The youngest pointed to their bare feet, and she waved at the two women.

As the final people were settling in for the service to begin, Katie's purse began singing the wedding song.

"What's that?" She held it up and looked at her purse blankly.

"Oh, here." Winnie grabbed it. "That's Jeffie. I re-set your ringer at the restaurant. You want to get this call." She pulled the phone out and handed it to Katie. The song was louder outside of the purse, and those closest to them were beginning to turn and stare.

"How do you know . . ." Yet, there was his face on the front of the phone.

"Out. Services are starting. Go, Sweetie." Winnie pushed Katie up and out of the pew.

Moving quickly, so as to minimize the disturbance,

Katie swiped the answer icon and pressed the phone to her ear, whispering, "Jeff?"

"Katie! I'm between services, and I hoped to get you. Are you free to talk just for a minute?"

"Yes, always." She was in the foyer by then, and the greeters were shutting the doors. One put her fingers to her lips, and Katie nodded, moving to stand as far from the doors as possible. "I'm in the vestibule, and the services are just getting started. Winnie's inside already. I don't want to make you late." She laughed, glad to hear his voice. She'd needed to hear his voice, and with this being her second service of the morning, she now understood why God had arranged to get her to the 9:00. He knew Jeff was going to call, and this way she could enjoy both.

"I'm in a pinch, Katie, and I need your help." His next words were muffled as if he had the receiver covered. "In a minute, Roker. I'm taking care of it now."

"Jeff, what's wrong?" Katie was growing more concerned by the moment.

"It's Janine. Remember I was headed out there last night?"

"Of course. What?" What now, was what she was thinking. Had Al run off? Had one of the boys set the house on fire? Poor Janine had seemed pretty frazzled a month ago when Katie had last seen her.

"Can you meet her there in town? Al's coming, but it'll be late tonight."

"Sure." But she thought, in Boston? Why would Janine be all the way down in the city? "Will she have the kids with her?"

"Nah, no kids." He covered the phone again and called, "Thirty more seconds and I'll be there. Have them sing one more song."

"Jeff. What is this about?"

"Sorry, Katie. I'm needed. You know, a one-horse show. Mass General at two. She should be there by then. She'll appreciate a familiar face. I love you, Katie, so very much. Coming, Roker." The phone went dead.

Katie supposed the final words weren't for her.

Janine, though, and Mass General. Why in the world would Janine be heading to the hospital in Boston without Al, and the kids . . . and it hit her, was Jeff babysitting again? Would he expect her to take up that job after they were married?

She slipped into her seat beside Winnie, her phone this time definitely off. She set it on the cushioned bench beside her, right between her and her friend.

"Did you like the ring tone?" Winnie leaned in and whispered. "I set it just for Jeff's number. I thought you would like that."

"Janine. I'm meeting her at the hospital." Katie said it in a whisper, the words making it real.

"In Maine?" Winnie's eyes were wide. "She's the one with the kids, right? That's hours away."

"No, here. Mass General."

"Hm. They're driving all the way down? Bangor has a hospital, don't they? Or Portland. That's even closer."

"I don't know. I'm supposed to be there at two. I don't even know what's wrong." It couldn't be good,

78

though. Winnie was correct. There were lots of good hospitals between Rockhaven and Boston. What could be so wrong that Janine was coming all the way to Boston? Only the highest priority cases came directly to Mass General.

She was distracted by the congregational reading. She was glad it was the same, and she took more comfort in it than this morning. Somehow, she felt it would be important to Janine, also, and she thought of her friend heading to Boston as the people started to rise around her.

She stood, and she took Winnie's hand as she began, "The Lord is my shepherd, I shall not want . . ."

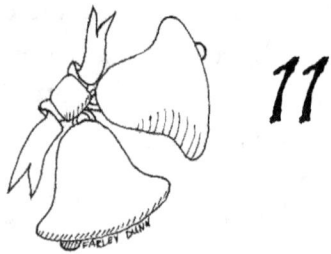

11

"The Children's Hospital. Are you sure? I don't think she's bringing any of her children with her."

Katie held her phone in her hand, messing with it, the screen blank, and wanting to call Jeff for clarification, but urgently feeling the need to be dependable Katie, self-sufficient Katie, the Katie who would do what she was asked in a moment of extreme emergency. It had always worked for her at ALDMass, but she was having trouble with it this afternoon.

"Yes. Even if she has no children, she will be arriving there. All MedFlight and other helicopter services use the helipad at the Children's Hospital." The well-dressed and very polite woman behind the information desk pulled out a map of the Mass General campus. "We are here, and if you follow this arrow—" She had a marker out, drawing in a path. "—it will take you directly there. Two o'clock, you say?"

"By two, I think." Katie wasn't entirely sure, because she wasn't entirely certain why she was here, only that she hadn't been able to get Jeff on the phone after services, and on the way to the hospital with her good friend Winnie in tow, she'd received a text that Janine would be arriving via helicopter. Helicopter! That sounded serious.

The woman—Brendy Barkie, she'd introduced herself earlier—glanced at a large clock on the wall. "I'm not sure you can get there by two. If you don't mind waiting a moment, let me make a call for you." She placed her hand on a phone and smiled at Katie, waiting on her response.

Katie nodded, and the woman picked up the receiver and turned away to begin the call.

Katie stepped to the lounge area, coming up behind Winnie and tapping her on the shoulder. Winnie turned, and seeing it was Katie, she grabbed her hand and pressed it to her face.

"Oh, Sweetie, was it bad? This, and I have to be gone all week, and you with your wedding plans all in a jumble. How will you make it through?"

"The receptionist is checking." Katie sat beside Winnie, reclaiming her hand, and holding her phone in front of her. "Nobody's answering, and that's what I can't figure out. I'm worried."

"Maybe it's simple, like appendicitis. Snip, snip, and she's all better." Winnie smiled brightly as she reached to pat Katie's knee. "Isn't Janine your reception go-to girl? She won't let you down."

81

"She may not have a choice." Katie looked away, squeezing the phone in her hands. Winnie, God bless her, wasn't making this easier. What she said was correct. Winnie was abandoning her, and Katie depended on her, beyond what Winnie knew. And the wedding. Sometimes she thought she had it all together in her head, the scheduling and the different people to organize to come together all on the same day; and then something would glitch up, and she felt it all coming undone.

Now this with Janine. She was, too, just what Winnie had described—her go-to girl—although Katie hadn't thought of it that way. Katie had been hesitant at first, her friend having to work around four wild island boys at home, but Janine had insisted. "It's something to do that's just mine, and I'll enjoy it, and don't you try to stop me." She had said it with such fervor that Katie had understood. Janine had drawn a line with her family, and she had claimed a slice of her time for her own.

Now, if something had happened to Janine—and it seemed it had—all that her friend was doing filled up Katie's vision until she could see nothing else. The chairs to be set up at the reception, the island women to be organized, even the on-island lodging for those from the city, Katie had let all that slide onto Janine's shoulders, and now she felt it sliding right back. It wasn't a feeling she liked, either.

"Miss?" It was Brendy from the information desk.

"You have news?" Katie stood, and out of the corner of her eye, she saw Winnie do the same.

"We do have a flight coming in. It's a few minutes early, so it's probably too late for you to get all the way there. From north of Portland. Your friend is coming out of Maine, correct?"

"Rockhaven. That's off the coast." Katie licked her bottom lip, her uncertainty making her jittery. "I guess she's coming directly from the island."

"No matter." The woman smiled warmly. "It's our only emergency transport from Maine today, so it's bound to be the correct one. Come with me, and I'll get you a new map. We'll get you and your friend connected."

"Thank you."

"You are very welcome." The receptionist reached a hand to Winnie. "Let me introduce myself before we go any further. I'm Brendy Barkie. How are you, today? Will you be meeting our new arrival, also?"

"I'm so sorry." Katie shook her head, embarrassed at her blunder. She hadn't introduced the two women. "Mrs. Barkie, this is Winnie Catron, my best friend forever. Winnie, Mrs. Barkie, my salvation in time of need."

Brendy chuckled. "Hardly your salvation, but thank you. Feel free to call me Brendy. I'm very glad to meet you, Winnie."

"You, too, Brendy." Winnie took her hand in both of hers, squeezing it for a moment before letting it go.

"Brendy. You told me that." Katie looked away. "I'm sorry. It's . . . I'm distracted, I guess."

"This is a distracting time. Don't you worry yourself about my name. Your friend, though." Brendy had been looking closely at Winnie. "Have we met, before? At a hospital reception or something?"

"I don't think so," Winnie said brightly. "But I'm glad to meet you now."

"I'm sorry. I know what I'm thinking." Brendy apologized. "You look like someone from the Macy's circular. It's not you, though. The girl in the ad has strawberry hair. Otherwise, the two of you could be twins."

"Twins?" Winnie's eyes sparkled. "Hear that, Katie? I could have a twin."

"Dear God, preserve us from the evil that might come our way." Katie felt lighter, though. Like she could get through Janine's trauma, as long as she had her good friend Winnie at her side.

"Oh, it's time." Brendy reached to touch a device on her waist that displayed a blinking red light on top. "They're on the pad and headed in. Let me check and see where you need to meet your friend. Excuse me for a moment."

It turned out Janine wasn't alone. Mass General had an outstanding oncology department that was second to none, able to diagnose and treat the most severe cancers, keeping alive those that other facilities had already written off, and easing the final days for the poor souls that were beyond the help of modern medicine.

The transport had come from Portland, and from Rockhaven, too. Janine was with her father, a man solidly in his fifties, and—his family had thought—in robust health. Indigestion that wouldn't be tamed, then uncontrollable and severe cramping had forced him to Portland. The cause behind the indigestion was what now had him in the hands of the good doctors at Mass General, the best hospital by anyone's measure in all of New England.

Janine was a mess when Katie and Winnie met up with her. Tears ran down her face, and she held a soaked tissue in one hand, with the pocket of her sweater filled with still more. The other hand held a near-empty tissue box that was growing lighter by the moment.

"Katie," she wailed, throwing her arms out. "They've taken Daddy to die! It's already metastasized, and there's nothing we can do!"

"Metastasized?" Winnie mouthed the word to Katie over Janine's sobbing form.

Katie shrugged, making a face to show she wasn't familiar with the word. Right then, the only thing she was interested in was giving Janine all the support she could. And right then, she clearly needed all she could get.

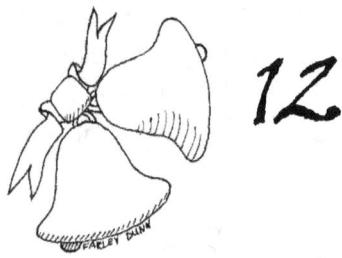

12

"No, I won't even listen to that." Katie held the third box of tissues out to Janine, and as her friend pulled one out, emptying it, Katie glanced inside to be sure, and she set it beside the trash bin. The bin was already overflowing, probably because it was entirely too small for grieving relations come to see dying loved ones in a cancer ward.

"I'm supposed to be helping, though." Janine blew her nose raggedly, wiping at it several times before dropping the tissue onto the already filled bin. "I mean, I can't leave Daddy, and I'm supposed to be up there getting all your *things* organized. Tables, chairs . . . the island guest lists. I haven't even started those. What will you do without me? I could scream!" She leaned her head back and pumped her hands up and down in frustration.

"It'll get done. You worry about your father, because he's all that matters now."

"It was going to be perfect. Island flowers on every table, only to complement the ones you ordered, of course." Janine sat up, her eyes shining with enthusiasm now, instead of pain. "I called the florist, you see, and I've been driving around with the boys. The boys!" She laughed, and it was infused with a tinge of hysteria.

"Were they helpful?" Katie thought not, but her friend needed gentle fingers just now, and to criticize would be to abrade already frayed emotions.

"You know my boys. Helpful as in not. But I did it, pretending we were just on a day jaunt in the car. If I'd let them know what I was looking for, they'd have found a way to trample them all down."

"No. They're better than that." However, Katie remembered a stolen rowboat, and one of Janine's boys claiming Katie had told him to take it, even with her standing directly in front of him. Kevie, she thought. They were toots, and there was no calling that horse by any other color.

"You spent time with them, but thank you. I just . . . this has been good for me, helping you out. It's like old times when we used to do things together. I looked forward to you coming every summer. You were fun, and the gang got together again. It wasn't the same after you left in September."

"Wasn't the same, how?" Got together *again*? They were together all winter, or at least that's the way Katie had always imagined it. It's what she'd envied when she'd sailed away on the last ferry of the summer.

Maybe island life was a two-pronged fork. Maybe the summer folk brought something to the island that they didn't realize, because it was always there when they were present. Some form of authenticity, like they validated the island when they showed up each summer. Their arrival told the islanders that people *remembered* them, and for some islanders—though not all, Katie was absolutely confident—the first summer people were a social waypoint marking the end of a long and sometimes harsh winter, with long nights and very short days.

Odd, she'd never thought of it that way, always imagining summer escapades that surely stretched over the winter months, when even for island children, there were days of unending rain, school, and chores to do before darkness ate the sky at 3:30 or 4:00 each afternoon.

She shivered at the realization, even as Janine went on.

". . . and that was Babe's problem, anyway, having nothing to do all winter. She told me the summer before your gramma's house burned that if she had to get pregnant, she was getting off the island."

"No." And Katie had felt so sorry for her. Surely it hadn't been intentional.

"Well, she's never been back, and both her parents still live up on the Reach. It's why she was so wild every summer. She said she had to cram nine months of living in three, because the rest of the months on the island weren't worth living." Janine sat back, her burst of energy deflating fast. "I understand now, with four boys under the same roof for six months. I dread rainy days, you know. I try not to watch the forecasts too closely, because I'm depressed two days before, and when it's over, I'm depressed for two more days, because I have to spend at least that long cleaning up the mud the boys tramped in."

"And here you are, with your father at a moment's notice. You are amazing, Janine Peavey. Al is so lucky. Your father is so lucky." Katie laughed, holding one finger up for emphasis, pointing it Janine's direction, and looking intently at her friend.

Janine squeezed Katie's wrist in thanks, giving her a brief smile, but the conversation had wound down, and they sat in silence for a time. Katie thought of her own parents, and wrapped up with them were memories of her grandmother.

She had loved her grandmother immensely, but going to the island each summer had been a tug of war emotionally. Oh, she wanted to go, but her parents thought differently. One year they had argued, with yelling and harsh words, and she had boarded the bus north in tears, vowing never to return to her parents ever again.

Of course, she had. Her home was Massachusetts, not Maine. Her school and her friends were all there, and after cooling down for several weeks, her grandmother had convinced her to call her parents and settle matters between them.

Then, after Carver House and her grandmother

were gone, there had been a new round of disagreements, her parents taking the side of mainland life, and Katie wanting to return to Maine. It hadn't worked out, though, and her northern world had been lost to her for a decade and a half. Funny, she'd always imagined the others living on as they had before, perhaps missing her, but doing all the things they'd done together as they grew up on their wild Maine island.

Then her father, older than those of her friends, with Katie being a late-in-life surprise, had developed a cough. Three months later he was bedfast, and her mother didn't last much longer. Somehow, with the home place sold to cover the final medical bills, she'd finally found time to go through all the old paperwork as the auction crew carried the last of her parents' things away. It seemed, although Katie had never imagined it at the time, her parents hadn't planned on her—or any children—and her birth had put a twist in their early retirement and travel plans.

Maybe that was the reason for their emotional distance from Carver Point. Grandmamma had lived the life they lost when she was born.

Katie couldn't undo what was done, and Janine still had her father. She patted her on the knee, and when her friend looked at her and smiled, Katie told her she would be here as long as she needed her, and excused herself to the ladies' room.

There, she looked in the mirror, and she splashed water on her face, pulling a paper towel to pat the remaining droplets clear. She peered deep into her eyes, wondering how prophetic Janine's words were. *What will you do without me?* What would she do without her? Most brides had a mother to help them plan, or a sister . . . a cousin, maybe. Katie had none of those. There was Nicolette, but she wasn't going to be much help, not all the way from France.

It was hitting home to Katie how much she had come to depend on poor Janine, just accepting her offers of help, without thinking of the cost to her time, or how much it must pull from her family. And Al, injured last month in that horrific wreck. How was he taking Janine's commitment to Katie's wedding?

"How are you going to do this, Katie?" She peered into her eyes, as if the person on the other side of the mirror was able to give her an answer that would springboard her off in a new direction. "Fifteen miles of ocean, and now I've lost Janine's help. How am I going to do this?"

She noticed her change of pronouns. The girl in the mirror? She was just a reflection of the little girl who'd wanted to live forever in her summer island life, and now she was getting the chance. Only thing, every pothole possible was getting in her way.

Was God trying to tell her something? Was she not paying attention?

"Katie?" There was a gentle knock on the door. "I don't mean to bother you, but I just got a call."

"One sec!" Katie brushed her hair back with her fingers, and she practiced smiling brightly. Turning, she opened the door, to see Janine was standing behind one of the waiting room chairs, tapping it gently and looking around the ceiling. She had a cell phone in one hand, but it looked off.

"There you are." Janine turned. Her eyes were red, but she smiled. "You are so beautiful."

"Okay. I don't know what that means, but tell me about the call. Was it good?"

"Well, Al's just outside the city, heading in. I thought you would like to know Jeff's with him." She smiled again, but it fell away, and she wiped a thumb under one eye.

"It's going to be okay." Katie put her hands on her friend's shoulders, then she pulled her close and hugged her for a moment, before releasing her with a short laugh. "You've got people who love you, and everything will be just fine."

"I know. I need Al here, that's all. If he gets here, I can make it through this. Really I can."

The news that Jeff was also arriving had turned Katie's thoughts around. She was completely on board with Janine, too. If Jeff were here, she could make it through this. Really, really she could.

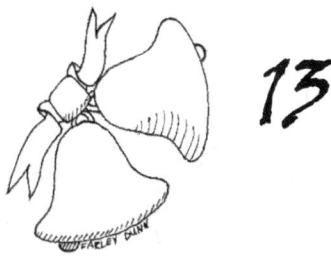

13

Winnie had long since evaporated, off packing for the Caribbean, and Janine was in with her father. Katie didn't know him well, other than as the occasional presence in his daughter's long-ago life, and she had encouraged her friend to spend some private time with the man she rarely saw anymore.

Katie took a deep breath. Poor Janine. From the looks of things, every minute she spent with him could be the last one. How could her own wedding woes hold a candle against what that broken-hearted woman must be going through?

At the window, she placed her hand against the glass. The rain had stopped, although the sun was still wrapped in fistfuls of ominous clouds. When cars passed on the street below, she caught bright, reflected images in the puddles still lingering along the curbs.

Glimpses, really, no more. There would be a bright flash of color and chrome, gone before she could really see it, and only recognizable because of the car speeding away.

Those that moved slower allowed her to see them better, her eyes catching with more clarity that wavering shimmer in the puddles that told of what was passing by at just that moment.

Those cars were her life, she mused, as she studied the way her hand left misty imprints on the glass when she moved it away. Through the damp and opaque residue, the world outside looked like a misty Rockhaven morning, with everything that was truth covered up by the fantasy that only the softening of a morning fog could lay across the land.

She had spent a week just months ago rediscovering a boy she'd known fourteen years before, and she'd learned the love she'd hoped for back then was still alive and waiting on her. That week had been a bright flash of shimmering chrome and richly hued paint against the asphalt and concrete that had made up her days.

Then, further down the road she'd caught glimpses of what her life with Jeff might be like in phone calls and letters, and the occasional weekend when they were able to get together to reforge that connection. The distance between each puddle was quite far, though, with the travel time from Boston to Rockhaven.

She recalled running out of the restaurant that morning on the way to service with Winnie. The rain had started to pound, and there was water everywhere: the sidewalks, the streets, even filling the drains along the curbs. Of course, filling the drains. It had been everywhere.

The only thing was that she hadn't been able to see any reflections at all. Oh, shards of this or that, but it was all broken up so quickly, that no one could have made anything of the images seen there. The water had covered everything, but nothing had reflected the world as it was. Rather, it was chaotic, a frightening world in disarray, where one could reach and grab at what might be out there, but only if one could find what the water was reflecting.

The puddles now were fewer, but they reflected more accurately. In them she could see bits of buildings, and the occasional limb of a tree. It wasn't much, but it was real, what was actually there, and not what one imagined to be there.

That was the way of life, Katie supposed. No, not supposed. She knew it. When life was happening, it was chaotic, sometimes fun, and often like the rain had been that morning. She and Winnie had stepped out of the restaurant, aware of the damage the falling torrent could do, and they had tried to protect themselves from the worst of it. Then, they had given in, and running across the street, they had become drenched with all the "life" that surrounded them.

They had laughed and had a good time, but only because "life" had come at them so unexpectedly, and they had refused to let it trap them. They had gone for broke. They had taken off their shoes and simply gone for broke, pedal to the metal, firing both barrels at the same time.

Katie thought of herself the past weeks, and she saw herself for the first time in a long time as she really was. She had been looking in the small puddles, finding bits of memories in long-ago Rockhaven, here and there seeing her life with Jeff the way it might be, and she had tried to protect herself from the worst of it: the leaving her friends and her apartment; moving for a lifetime to a new and only partially familiar island; and inserting herself into the everyday existence of people to whom Boston was a nightmare from the other side of the world.

"Katie, Katie," she whispered. "You want everything to be picture perfect, and it's not, ever. Life comes at you, messy and unpredictable, and you have to just jump in and hope you can swim. A life jacket never hurts, though." She smiled and thought of Jeff. He made a pretty good life jacket. At least she expected he would.

She reached down and pulled off her shoes, holding them in one hand. She wriggled her toes, remembering the rain. She wanted to run barefoot, with Jeff, of course, but barefoot, nonetheless. Leap into the rain, and laugh with abandon as life dumped itself on her head, bathed in a wild torrent of happiness at times, and the crashing maelstrom of disappointment at others. No little puddles for her! She wanted the whole shebang. She held her arms out and twirled in the silence of the empty room.

"Katie? What are you doing?" Janine stood across

the room with a wad of tissues in one hand.

Katie froze, remembering her shoes held in one hand, and Janine's awful predicament on the other. Her face warmed. "Being an idiot. I'm sorry."

"I know. You've got to relieve the stress someway. I tell Al now and then I've got to go into the woods where no one can see me and scream. He laughs, but I mean it sometimes. Your idea is much better. Take off your shoes and dance." Her face screwed up again, and she pressed the tissues to her eyes. "I'm sorry. It's Daddy. They can't give me any good news at all. I need Al."

"Oh, Janine." Katie tossed her shoes to the floor and dashed to throw her arms around her friend. "Al's on the way. Come sit. There's only one thing you can do. Give it to God."

"I know. Jeff says that all the time in services. Give it to God. What if God doesn't give it back?" She shook with emotion, sobbing, even as she let Katie seat her on one of the sofas.

"We can't control that. We let go, and God does what He knows is best. So, let's take hands, and if you don't mind, I'll pray, and you listen to what God says to you in your heart."

"You're right." Janine sniffled. "Daddy's had a good life. He's been a bear, never sick, so I suppose if he had to linger, it'd be harder for him than this. Maybe God knows what He's doing in spite of my complaints."

"That's it. Now, here I go. Father, Holy One, we know you hear our prayers . . ."

As she prayed, Katie knew it was true, because about halfway through, unseen to Janine, in walked Al, followed by Jeff. Al started to walk forward, and when he saw the prayer, he stopped, removing his hat and holding it stiffly in his hands. Jeff put his hand on his friend's shoulder, and he dropped his eyes in respect.

"Amen." Katie finished up, and she grabbed Janine in a hug. She looked her in the eyes and said, "How do I know I can trust God? Because during our prayer, He answered it with something you really need. Al just walked in the door."

"Al! Oh, Al, I've needed you here so much!" With the fountains gushing forth once again, Janine turned from Katie, and she ran to throw herself against her husband.

"You're a good woman, Dame Carver." Jeff kissed her on the forehead as he stepped to her and put one arm around her.

"And I told you I'd push you overboard if you kept calling me that." It felt good to have him at her side, teasing her, like everything was going to be all right. "I need a real hug, Jeff. It's been a long day."

"I've got one to give." He wrapped his arms around her, and he picked her up and swung her around in a full circle before setting her down. "You seem shorter than usual today. What's that about?"

Katie laughed. "I'm shoeless. That's worth at least two inches."

"Ah, shoeless. That explains everything." He struggled against a laugh, as if it didn't explain anything at all.

"The rain, Jeff. You have to take off your shoes in the rain." She patted him on the chest. "You never, never wear your shoes in the rain." She knew she was being silly, but she was giddy with him in her arms.

"That really explains everything. Rain in the hospital waiting room. Maybe I should suggest Al transfer his father-in-law to a better facility."

"Don't you dare. Janine's barely holding it together as it is. Let me get my shoes on."

She moved to pick them up only to see a nurse come into the room. She stepped to Janine and spoke to her quietly. After a moment of discussion between the nurse and Al, the three of them exited the room.

"Think that's good or bad?" Jeff had slipped his hands in his pockets, and he made a face, questioning with his eyes.

"Depends on your point of perspective. From what I've picked up, the end of this tale will be very bad, indeed. This particular paragraph, well, I'm glad Al's here now. He's just what Janine's needed."

Katie had her shoes on by then, and she took a deep breath and let it out. A question had been flitting around in the back of her mind, one she hated to bring up, because it could undo carefully laid plans that might never come together again. Yet, she had to, if she wanted to live with herself.

"Jeff. About the wedding." She stopped, dreading the actual question, and finding the window easier to look out of. It was once again spattered with drops.

"What about it?" He placed his hand on her neck and stood at her side. "Wet out there. Not in here." He chuckled, glancing down at Katie's shoes.

"Should we, what with this about Janine's dad, think about it?"

"Think how?"

"You have to have considered this." She looked up to see him half smiling. "What? You have considered it. I can tell."

"What have I considered?" Still that half smile.

"Rescheduling. A funeral and a wedding that close." She shivered, as if saying it made it real. Janine could never hear her say that. Ever. It would be like a prediction.

"Al and I discussed it on the way down. We're not postponing."

"And if . . ." This was the worst of all. She gathered her determination and spat it out. "What if we have to have the funeral on the same day?"

"Like I said, we're not postponing. Al and I agreed, and he knows Janine will feel the same."

"All right, then." She placed her head against his shoulder. "Everything's on."

"It'll work out. You'll see." He put one arm all the way across her shoulders, and he squeezed her gently before relaxing to stand against her.

Katie wanted to hear Janine say that, though. It was easy for two men to make whatever decisions they wanted, but they weren't the ones losing their father. Janine was, and this was up to her. It was totally and unequivocally up to the one woman to whom today's events mattered most of all.

Then it hit her. Where were the boys?

"Jeff? Where are Al and Janine's kids?"

"Don't you worry about *that*." He laughed softly. "We farmed them out."

"You did, did you?" She remembered him doing that once before. It had worked pretty well, too. It seemed Jeff had a firm handle on just about everything that happened on Rockhaven.

Maybe things would go off without a hitch after all. If Jeff were there, then she'd trust him to pick up whatever pieces might come breaking off their finely crafted wedding plans.

It's what he was good at, after all.

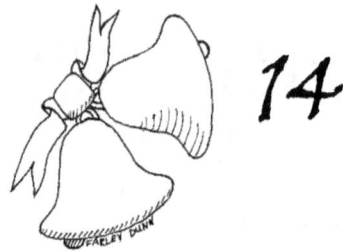

14

Monday dawned bright and clear.

According to the forecast, it would be hot, too. Boston hot, with stifling humidity and early morning traffic. The rain from Sunday had drenched lawns and patios, and all that water had to go somewhere. Once the early morning fog burned away, the sun would grab at the remains of yesterday's deluge and whip it into the air.

It would make the air a wall of water that one would need to swim through.

Katie began the experience while the rest of Boston was still snoozing on their favorite pillows. Winnie was her wake-up call at the unfathomable hour of five. She was off to the islands, she'd quipped, brighter and more chipper than Katie had imagined her friend could muster at such an early hour. She wanted to know how

Janine's father was doing, and when did he get out of the hospital? And, oh, did Jeffie come down, too? That was something he would do, because he was such a sweet man.

Katie barely found the answers. Groggily, her head still thick with sleep, she mumbled, "As well as can be expected; yes and no; and yes he did. And thank you. That's why we have a wedding planned."

"Okay, Sweetie. Let me know if anything changes." And she rattled off a phone number that probably belonged to the production company, telling Katie that her phone surely wouldn't work "way down there."

Katie sat up, her feet finding her slippers on the floor. The sofa was comfortable enough. It just wasn't her bed. She'd let Al and Janine have that. It was the only one she owned large enough for two. Upstairs? Jeff was ensconced there. He'd overnighted in the loft once before, and she refused to take that away from him.

She missed her bathroom, though. Yet, she didn't really mind giving it up. In a couple months, it wouldn't be hers, anyway. Someone else would be living in her Boston apartment. Why not start practicing now? More to the point, after the news Al and Janine had received at the hospital, they needed their privacy. And today, they had a decision to make. A very hard decision to make.

It wasn't Katie's, though, and she was glad enough for that. She grabbed up her toothbrush from the coffee table and spoke to it softly, "Thank you for joining me for the night. Come to the bathroom with me, and let's have a little early morning dance."

"Katie?"

She froze. She'd forgotten the loft opened to the living room, and the French doors must have been left open. Her and her big mouth. Why couldn't she keep it closed when other people were around to hear?

"You awake down there?"

"Hey, Jeff. Not really." That was God's truth.

"I didn't sleep well and heard something about a dance. You have company down there?"

"Only my toothbrush." She held it up in the dark, although she knew it was for her benefit, only. Jeff couldn't see it, unless he had Superman eyes. Then, after his masterful performance yesterday with Al and Janine, maybe he did.

A soft light flickered on in the loft, filtering across the living room ceiling, the glow one she recognized from a gift she'd received several years before. It was an egg that when touched shimmered with soft LEDs. It was on a timer that automatically shut off after ten minutes. Touch it twice, and you had light for twenty.

Twenty minutes, she thought. Just enough time to fall back asleep, if only I didn't have to go in to work today.

"Hey."

It was Jeff's warm voice again, and when she looked up, there he was, leaning over the railing, his hair rumpled and wild, and a roughened shadow of beard across his jaw. He was in plaid pajama bottoms with a paisley top. Oops, Katie thought. Al in the bedroom was probably matching, except Al would have

104

on a paisley bottom and a plaid top. She found that funny, and she began to giggle, looking away and covering her mouth.

"So, what's that about?" He yawned and rubbed one hand across his face, and in the same motion, he ran it through his hair, pushing it back from his forehead. It fell right back down, though, and he ignored it, as if he had actually made a difference, and the shock of hair was now right where he wanted it.

"You." She crossed her arms and looked up at him. "Did you even look at what you're wearing?"

He glanced down and pulled at the fabric of his pants, shaking his head. Then he pulled at his shirt. "Looks okay to me. You don't like paisley and plaid together?"

"Oh, paisley and plaid are just fine. It's that you and Al are twins. Depending on whether you like paisley or plaid, he has on your pants or your shirt."

"He does, does he?" Jeff had his elbows resting on the railing, and he looked down at her. His voice was soft and low, and he didn't act as if it were much of a problem. "And whose fault is that?"

Seeing him there, his face shadowed in the dim light, with only his voice floating so easily down to her, it was his shoulders that stood out. They were a man's shoulders, a working man's shoulders. A lobsterman's, to be exact. How could this man be so beautiful?

After too long a pause—way too long, Katie decided—she whispered, "Mine."

"So, I guess I can expect an apology." His words

were barely there as they returned to her, but they carried laughter woven into every syllable.

"You are a fool, Jeff Ragsdale. How do you expect me to apologize for mixing up your pajamas?" She would have laughed at him, except for Al and Janine just in the other room. And it was too early for any sane person to be awake, unless they were headed to some Caribbean island for the week.

"Oh, I could think of a few ways. That toothbrush. Are you planning on starting that dance anytime soon? When you're finished, I need to make my way down to your level."

"Oh, oh, right." She grimaced. She wasn't thinking. Four people. Two bathrooms. She didn't have the liberty to indulge staring at Jeff just because he was here. Today, this morning, her bathroom was meant for sharing.

"You go dance. Buzz me when you're through. Oh, and good morning, Katie. I don't get to say that very often to the woman I love." He turned, and gently pushing the French doors closed, he disappeared from view.

"Good morning, Jeff Ragsdale." She whispered it, too softly for anyone to hear. It was something she wanted to say every day, and she wanted to say it with a kiss to the man she loved.

It was a pretty good way to start a morning, she thought. A pretty good way indeed.

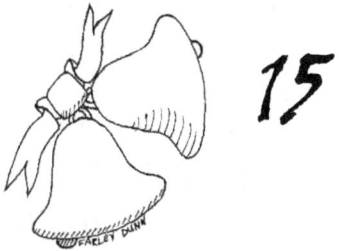

15

Katie hit the humidity when she exited through the glass doors of her apartment building. It smacked her in the face, and it wasn't even hot.

Yet.

It felt it, though. When she caught a ray of sun peeking through two buildings, it was a stab of bright heat across her dark blue blazer. For a moment she considered heading back to change, but then she remembered her bedroom was off limits, and she would be inside most of the day, anyway. All she had to do was walk a short distance, catch the T, and she could relax until late afternoon.

She would need to purchase a sandwich from the food cart, though, if she were out of soup in her desk drawer. Who knew after the hectic jumble of Friday's presentations?

At the stairs down to the T, she felt in her purse to make sure her personal phone was there and on. The hospital was awaiting a decision from Al and Janine on how long they wished to keep Janine's father on life support before letting nature take its course. Already he was unresponsive, and hospice care was their only option. He could go home, if Janine wished, or remain at Mass General for more personalized care.

That had been the final trauma of the evening. How does a person let go, when the week before, her father had been on a golf course, and hosting his partner to lunch at the club? Now, the doctors said the machines were the only reason he still lived.

Katie couldn't imagine, except that she could. Her father had gone in much the same way, only more slowly. She didn't envy Janine's day. Stay as long as you need, Jeff, she'd said before leaving the apartment. Make yourselves at home, and let Al and Janine sleep as long as they need. They're bound to be exhausted.

He was exhausted, he'd replied. But, yes, he would let them sleep, and they'd give Katie a call the first they heard something. He'd hugged her, kissing her ever so gently on the lips, and she'd pulled herself away. She didn't trust herself to stay. Somehow, she thought, maybe it was better he was on the island, and she was in Boston. She was too much in love with him to keep away. She was surviving by the two hundred miles in between. Any less distance, and like magnets, she'd let them be drawn together, never to be separated again.

This morning they were separated, though, as she was working, and he was keeping his friends' lives from falling apart. It was Lesly that Katie ran into first, coming out of the parking garage as she traversed the last of the sidewalks before entering the building.

"Hey, Les," she called, very brightly. "How was your weekend?"

"Busy, and that rain yesterday. Have you ever seen so many dogs and cats fall from one sky? I was glad I didn't have to get out. How about you?" Lesly held her keys in one hand, this time hers and not her husband's. "A couple more weeks, and you'll be hitched."

"I like to call it a merger. Two great corporations linking assets to become one." Katie smiled as she said it. After yesterday, it was good to step into a world that wasn't weighted down by an impending death and a best friend that had abandoned her in the middle of it all. It was nice to joke about something just for the joke's entertainment value.

"Nah. Not a merger. It's the tie that binds, so get ready for it. It's the tie that ties you down, if you want to know the truth." Lesly nodded knowingly.

"Is that a bad thing?" They were inside, where the humidity was cut in half, and Katie's blazer felt pleasantly warm.

"Not for Brian and me. It's the babies that do it. Kids? Wait as long as you can, if you want my advice." They greeted the receptionist before heading to the elevator. Once they were past, Lesly laughed. "If you want my advice, don't have them, but what kind of expert am I? I've got two, and a grandbaby on the way. So, don't listen to me."

Once in the main reception room for the claims adjustment division, Lesly waved as she headed off, saying she couldn't afford to clock in late. She'd see Katie at the morning staff meeting.

The wrapped box on her desk surprised Katie. She picked it up and opened the small card dangling from the ribbon. *Katie, Katie, Katie* was all it said.

"Hm," was her spoken response. There was no hint of who might have put it here. No suggestion of who might be waiting in the wings to catch her response, and she knew there must be someone watching. A prank, perhaps? She still remembered the keys from the previous Monday.

Stepping to the door, she looked up and down the corridor, and seeing no one, she worked her finger under the edge and broke the wrapping loose. If they were watching, she would see they got her response. "I'm opening the gift." She called the warning into the emptiness.

A voice she didn't recognize replied from far away, "If it's candy, I get a piece." Whoever it was laughed, as if they didn't really intend to claim the prize.

"That's what you think," she muttered. Katie, Katie, Katie. She tried to picture who at work had ever called her that, but she came up blank. She could only think of one possibility. This had to have been from three of her friends, joining in to buy her something extra special. It was obvious, one Katie for each of her coworkers.

Her anticipation building, she slipped the wrapping paper free, and she was left holding a brightly worked metal box. Pushing the clasp aside, she raised the lid and lifted it. "Oh," she said, sitting at her desk, and dropping her purse to the floor.

It was a small spiny sea urchin, brightly colored, with all the spines removed. She lifted it and turned it, seeing the bottom was plugged with a rubber stopper. Shaking it, it rattled softly, and the motion brought forth an exotic smell of roses and wild berries. She pulled a note from beneath it and unfolded it.

"Katie. This made me think of your island. Rockhaven's going to be your home, and I'll miss you so much. This is for your desk, so you'll remember Jeff misses you even more. All my love, Winnie, Winnie, Winnie."

Katie's eyes watered as she remembered what this was about. On her friend's first visit to Rockhaven, Winnie had exited the ferry, and they'd done just that, called each other's name multiple times in excitement.

Winnie, Winnie, Winnie, she thought. I'm going to miss you more than you can ever know. She cleared a spot at the edge of her desk, one right in the center, and she placed the sea urchin all by itself, just where everyone who came in to talk to her would see it.

"Knock, knock!" Katie's supervisor stood at her cubicle door, and she peered in, smiling brightly. She held a company tablet in one hand.

"Good morning, Connie. How was your weekend?" Katie stuffed the paper from the gift into the trash bin, and she set the box on the floor by her purse.

"Always good." She looked at her tablet, tapping on it once. "You're here, but don't forget to clock in. I know you're at your desk, but Corporate only knows if you say so on your computer. I see you got your gift all right. I'm glad. That was left with the night watchman this morning at the crack of midnight."

"Crack of midnight." That was funny. Katie laughed as she held up the sea urchin and shook it. "My good friend is on a photo shoot to the Caribbean. She gave me this. Smell."

"Wonderful." Connie inhaled deeply. "Roses. I thought people brought gifts when they returned from trips."

"This is from Rockhaven in July." Not exactly, but close enough. "From Macy's, most likely, but we find them on the island. It's to remind me of Jeff."

"Ah," and Connie nodded her head as if she understood. "Did you get to see him this weekend?"

"I certainly did. Thank you, Connie. I guess I should log in, now."

"Best, dear. We want to keep Corporate happy. Remember, staff meeting in fifteen minutes. Breakfast is provided, and most of your coworkers are already there." She tapped her tablet once more, smiled, and disappeared down the corridor.

Katie hadn't wanted to say that Jeff was still at her apartment. How would that look? It didn't matter that another married couple was with him, or that he was only there because of her friend's father, now dying in a local hospital. To explain all that would sound too much like a list of excuses, when all people would hear was that they had been in the same apartment overnight. Different beds and on different floors? They most likely wouldn't believe that part.

Well, that was the way it had happened. God believed her. But even Katie knew better than to trust her friends with that juicy bit of information.

Thinking of Al and Janine, she pulled her phone from her purse, and she placed it on her desk. Tapping it on, she checked it for missed calls or texts. Nothing. So, either Al and Janine were still sleeping, or they were making their decision as she sat here. She would keep the phone at the ready, even in the meeting, because she didn't want to miss a call this important.

She'd missed Jeff's call the week before. Look where that'd gotten her. She wasn't missing another one. This was her new life, coming to make her part of it. She planned to jump in with both shoes off. It was the only way to live life to its fullest, and that's exactly what she intended to do.

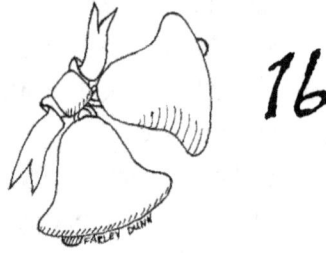 **16**

"You don't have to do this, Janine."

It was early morning, and it was cool for a change. The sun was creeping over the tops of the buildings, and before long, Katie would say good bye for a time to Al and Janine. Jeff had driven back to Maine the previous Monday, and Al and Janine had continued to claim Katie's bed.

Katie's heart went out to her friend, both for her sorrow and her unqualified generosity. Who else in the whole world could lose a father to an undiagnosed and rampantly aggressive disease, and not wallow in self-pity about it for weeks on end? Now her friend continued to insist that the entire reception was on her plate, and if Katie would let her, she wanted to help with the wedding, too, as much as she could manage from the island.

"I do, too, have to do this." Janine threw her arms around Katie, and she hugged her tightly. "If I don't have this wedding to plan, I'll go crazy." She backed away, sniffling, and she dabbed at her eyes with a tissue. "Once I get Daddy taken care of, then I'm leaping into your wedding with both feet. It's going to be the island event of the summer."

"Not so fast." Al had his one good arm around Janine by then. The other was still in a cast from the wreck he'd been in back in July. "We don't want to rush the love birds too much."

"Katie knows what I mean. Anyway, it's summer on the island until the first cold snap, and that won't come until October. I can call it whatever season I want, even if it is after the middle of September." Janine was finally smiling. She had made it clear this project captivated her, and her improving humor verified it.

"I see a bus arriving. You know, I could still drive you up."

"We'll be dropped off at the terminal door. I have my tickets, and this saves you a whole day behind the wheel." Al patted his breast pocket and smiled. "Anyway, you have work today."

"Give your boys my best, and when you see him, give Jeff my love." Katie took her friend's hand, and she squeezed it. Al was right, but Katie felt it necessary to at least offer. This afternoon was her shower at work. It had been planned for weeks, and to miss it? Even for this? Al and Janine had refused to allow her to think of it, especially after putting up with the two of them, Al had joked.

When the expected had happened, as bad as it was, at least it happened here, Al had remarked over coffee one evening, and not at home where Janine would be reminded of her father's demise at every turn. He had sipped the final dregs from his cup, and pointed at his wife through the bedroom door, curled up in exhaustion and finally asleep.

"Our boys," and he'd paused, looking out the windows at the shadows cast by the setting sun on the buildings across the street, "take a lot of energy, and Janine bears the brunt. After the second, we intended to stop, but things didn't work out that way. She's envied you, since you've been back. I appreciate you letting her do this for you, in spite of all that's happening now."

He'd taken a deep breath and stood, placing his cup in the sink, and making his way to his wife in the other room.

Katie had watched him go, not wanting to rob him of his moment. It wasn't like Al to be outspoken with her. He'd hardly said four words to her since she'd returned to the island in summer.

In summer. What a long time ago that seemed, her returning after fourteen years away, only having recently learned her grandmother's property had been willed to her, and all she had to do was claim it.

She'd claimed much more on that trip: time spent with Winnie; faded island friendships restored; and a fiancé, one who had grown handsomer with the years. It had only been weeks ago, and already it seemed so much time had passed. She knew what made the difference. It wasn't the time. It was what filled up the time, and hers had been very full since she'd returned from Rockhaven.

Now, she was sending Al and Janine back to Maine with Janine's heartfelt assurance that Katie had done more than she and Al could have asked. The funeral was to be no more than a private memorial, as her father's will stated he was to be cremated. He wanted his ashes tossed off the ferry as it traveled to the island. Not from, but to, like he was going home, forever caught up in the wake of the boat. When Janine had told her, the long-ago memory came to Katie. As a girl, she remembered Janine's father saying exactly that, thinking it was a macabre joke to send shivers up a young girl's spine. No. Janine assured Katie that her father had always said that's the way he wanted to go. She might one day put a marker for him in one of the island cemeteries, but there would be no one there. He would be in his sea, floating across the world forever.

"I could still come up for the ceremony. Please?" Katie hated thinking she was abandoning Janine, just sending her off, and not being there in her moment of closure.

"Al and I talked about that." Janine had her one small bag's long strap over her shoulder by then, and she squeezed Katie's arm. "Being here in peace and quiet—"

"Without the boys," Al interjected, with an awkward grin.

"Okay, Al. You don't have to explain it so bluntly. Katie understands. He means that without the boys we got to really talk. We want to wait until you're coming up for good. We'll ride the ferry off the island and back. You and Jeff, and the boys, too, can drop a little of Daddy off the side. That's probably all we can get away with, anyway. We don't want to cause a problem with the Transportation Authority."

"You are so sweet." Katie leaned in and kissed her on the cheek. "Have a good trip, and oh, be strong when you think of how much your father loved you all those years he lived on the island with you."

"Bye-bye, blushing bride." Janine giggled before climbing on the bus.

"I'll tell Jeff how much you miss him." Al winked and climbed aboard after her.

It was hard watching the bus drive away, but then it was easier, too. It was just . . . just Katie, then. No Al, no Janine, no Winnie, and no Jeff. She was back in her element, with her blue Bug, her trendy apartment, and her very stable job at ALDMass. For the first time all week, she had a few minutes to herself, and maybe, just maybe she could get back on track with her wedding plans. In spite of Janine's generous offer, there was stuff only Katie could do.

With Winnie, of course, to call on in the tight spots.

Her purse began singing to her, and she frowned, opening it and pulling out her phone. Certain it was Connie, and trying to recall if she'd remembered to let her know she would be late this morning, she held it to her face and answered.

"Katie, here. I'm on my way. Sorry."

"Oh, Sweetie, how'd you know I even needed a ride? How long until you're here?"

"Winnie? Is that you?" Logan! Katie knew that's where her friend would be.

"Of course, Sweetie. Who else would call you at this time of the morning? Did you like my little present?" She sounded tired, but her voice was chipper, anyway.

"Everyone's loved it. It sits right on my desk." What was on the tip of her tongue was something else, though. She was thinking, If you expected me to give you a ride, shouldn't you have let me know? What she said was, "I'm headed to the car. I'm at the Greyhound Terminal, so it won't be long."

"Oh, you're so silly, and that's why I love you so much. But Sweetie, that was a senseless place to wait for me. I couldn't ride the bus all the way across the ocean. Greyhound might be good, but not even they can walk on the water. We'll save that for Jesus." She giggled. "Once you get here, I'm planning to sleep all afternoon. See you in a bit!"

And the line went dead.

Well, Katie thought. So much for Winnie helping out in the tight spots. Rather, she was a tight spot, one that was waiting on her at Logan Airport.

Still, she had what she had, and that little sea urchin had been a nice treat all week long. Every time she felt Janine's father bringing her down, she had shaken her urchin and enjoyed the smell of roses and berries. It had reminded her of Carver Point, and that had reminded her of Jeff.

That was her goal, after all, Jeff and the island. Of course, she couldn't have one without the other, but that was the point, wasn't it? Jeff and the island, forever and ever, amen.

That made her smile as she put her key in the ignition and started her little Beetle up. She imagined what Winnie would be saying if Janine and Al had taken her up on her offer to drive them to Maine.

"Katie, Katie, Katie!" She could picture her friend now.

And her reply? It would be what it always was: "Winnie, Winnie, Winnie!"

Winnie would never change, and Katie felt somehow better knowing that. Her friend was the one constant she had depended on forever, and she was glad to claim her as her number one favorite person.

Right under Jeff, of course, but right up there with the best.

After all, those three words sounded the same in any language.

"Winnie, Winnie, Winnie!"

Katie laughed as she pulled out into the street, not even caring that the parking attendant looked at her strangely as she drove away.

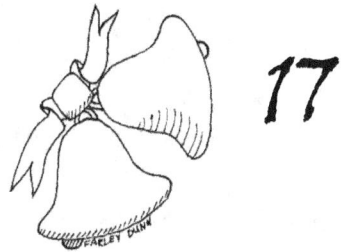

17

Katie held her list of things to do in one hand, and a retractable pen in the other. It was an important list, the most vital one she'd ever made.

The shower the previous Friday at ALDMass had been just what her friends had suggested, a charming meet-and-greet. More of a cake-and-punch social, with the social outweighing the shower. The reason was that ALDMass was huge, and she didn't know well many of those there that day. A collection had provided a money tree, and it was appreciated, but it didn't compare to the more intimate shower given by her friends at Friday's.

Outside the windows of her apartment, the late-afternoon sun washed the distant buildings, catching her attention. The windows were open to let in the perfect September breeze, and she pressed the paper against the tabletop, setting a thin book on top to keep it from blowing to the floor.

She laid the pen on the table beside it, glad to have the afternoon off. The sun might have warmed the sidewalk, but the air carried hints of the upcoming season. The two together? Priceless.

"This is a day to die for." The words came from the loft. "Hey! Yoo-hoo, down there. Why aren't we out there soaking up some rays?"

"Because I have a job," Katie called up. To herself she muttered, "Unlike some lucky people." Winnie did have a job, but it was sporadic, giving her plenty of time to play. Modeling paid well, but sometimes she had weeks between assignments. Such was the price of being naturally wonderful, her friend had quipped on more than one occasion.

"For one more day. That's not so bad." Winnie adjusted one of the jeweled combs in her hair, pulling the ebullient mass back from her face. "I'll be right down."

"And I'll put you to work. Are you sure?"

Winnie laughed and waggled her fingers over the rail. With a jangle of spangles on her arms and neck, she disappeared. It was only a second before she reappeared down the stairs. She walked to the windows to stand in the breeze. Her thick and permanently curled hair lifted in the inrush of warmed air, a strawberry halo against her permanent tan.

"You are so beautiful. How do you do it?" Katie put her chin on her palm, and rested her elbow on the table. Of course, beautiful was the reason the girl got so many modeling gigs. She was a fairy princess of unimaginable good fortune. Now all she needed was a Prince Charming of her own to have it all.

"Good genes." Winnie looked at Katie and smiled, her bright teeth lighting up her face. "The elliptical trainer at the gym helps, too, and one day, liposuction!"

"Lipo-what? I can't see you ever needing that." Katie picked her list back up, the beautiful spell broken. It was just Winnie, lovable and inscrutable Winnie, and that was all right, if sometimes irritating. Not too much so, though. She smiled at that.

"What's funny?" Winnie pursed her lips as if petulant, but her eyes laughed as she spoke.

"Look at this." The list made a good distraction. "Maybe I should call Jeff and tell him March is a better time for a wedding."

"Girl!" Winnie picked up the list and shook it, rattling the paper, and completely ignoring Katie's suggestion. "You have got to get to hopping. That knot's not going to tie itself. I may actually have to take over some of these for you."

"No, you don't. I will not have Donatella Designs doing my wedding." Katie snatched the list back from Winnie. "Besides, I'm not rich enough to afford anything you'd want to do."

"Donatella Designs." Winnie giggled. "There's no such firm anywhere that I've heard of. When did you become the fashion expert? Now, someday I might have a little shop and call it Winnie's Designs. Think you'll be able to afford what I do?"

"Seriously. Real designers don't give away their goods." Katie knew the better stores often let Winnie have what she wore in the shoots, but designers? Ha, was her thought on that.

"Oh, I don't know. People like me, and I can pull a few favors, if I put my mind to it." Winnie sat and smirked. She tapped the paper on one particular entry. "You can mark this one off. I've taken care of this already."

"The bridesmaids' dresses?" It was an entry that was starred. Katie had thought it was all wrapped up, and it had come apart at the seams once again. All her best friends at work were to be on Rockhaven, attired in identical outfits, the design selected from a Macy's line that was as affordable as Katie could stomach, yet when she'd mentioned it casually to Lisa Vickers the previous Monday, her coworker had looked at her in surprise. "The Macy's dress? Oh, friend, I am so glad you let Winnie take over that little detail. No offense, but . . ." and she had wrinkled her nose and shaken her head. Then Connie had paged Katie, and she hadn't found out what Lisa meant.

That's why it was on the list.

"You don't need to worry, Sweetie." Winnie smiled impishly and tapped Katie on the nose with one finger. "Everything will match beautifully. And I get to wear vintage Oscar. I'm so excited!"

"De la Renta?" Katie choked. She might not wear high fashion, but she knew the names of the best designers. "No one in this wedding party can afford that. Remember, we're working girls, not debs out to spend

Daddy's money."

"That's why you have me. As I told you, I've taken care of this already. Now, where's a pen?" She picked up the one Katie had laid down earlier, and she clicked the end. With a flourish, she squiggled a line across the page, right through Katie's reminder to find out just what was going on with the attendants' dresses.

Katie took a moment to breathe deeply before responding. "Do I get to see what everyone's wearing?"

"Sweetie, if it's Oscar, you *know* it'll be fabulous. So, you don't worry one minute. You can trust your good friend, Winnie, don't you know? I have never let you down, not once, not ever. Now, before this evening gets away, let me see those hands." Winnie grabbed Katie's hands and began to inspect her fingernails. "Ole Brandywine. Do you ever wear anything else? Oh, well, it'll go with the dress I've picked out for you, so I guess it's okay. This one's chipped, though, so I need to get busy. At least they've grown out from all that damage you did back in July. You butchered these, Sweetie, and I thought your nails were lost forever!"

Katie gave in as Winnie pulled her obviously prepared manicure supplies from a small bag beside the table, and proceeded to happily begin repairing any damage she could find.

However, Katie was pretty sure she had already picked out a dress. She had gone to a fitting at a good but moderately priced shop, although it wasn't paid for yet. The wedding was two weeks away, and with tomorrow her last day at work, she'd planned on getting all the final strings tied together in what she'd come to call her "Detail Week."

"Where's your Brandywine?" Winnie said it absently as she applied filler to one rough nail. The other hand soaked in polish remover. "We're going for a full fresh coat."

"My Brandywine?" Katie shook her head as she rolled her eyes. "You're the manicurist. You figure it out."

"Oh, girl, why do I have to do everything around here?" Winnie set her tools aside, and she stood. "Now, you don't move. You and me? We've got some major repairs going on, and we can't scrimp on this. Tomorrow's your big day, and we want you to go out with a bang."

"With a bang?" Katie smiled.

"Like in a western. Be back with a nice bottle of *po-losh,* quick as a rattler on a rat." She giggled.

"Po-losh? Say it correctly, polish, and what's this rattler on a rat all about?"

"My new photo shoot coming up. It's for a western store. You like that? Sczz-zz-zz." She made a sound like a rattlesnake before disappearing into the bedroom.

Katie was sitting with one hand soaking and the other covered with drying filler when her phone rang. "Winnie? My phone's beside the bed. Can you get it?"

"I'm under the sink. Give me a minute." Her reply was faint, as if she truly was under the sink. The phone had stopped ringing when she returned from the bedroom with it in her hand.

"Was it Jeff?" It was about time for him to call.

"Let's see." Winnie smiled and tapped the play icon.

"Hey, Katie. Jeff here. Busy week." He laughed in the recording. "Out to collect the boys from school. Some after-school something. Detention, probably. Al's at the clinic getting his cast off. Love you."

"Call him back." Ooh! That Winnie! Katie had her hands totally tied up, and there was nothing she could do about it.

"Let's see. I think the number's 1-800-J-E-F-F-I-E. Oh. Not enough numbers." She looked at Katie and tittered. "Maybe it's 1-800-L-O-V-E-J-E-F-F. Oh, that's too many."

"Oh, you. If I had my hands free . . ." Katie growled.

"Oh, I'm scared now. Okay." Winnie tapped the phone. "Now it's ringing. Now. Now. Oh, it's a recording. Wait on it . . ."

"Hold it closer." Katie wanted Jeff to hear her apology for missing his call.

Winnie seemed to think otherwise.

"Hey, Jeffie. Katie's on the other side of the room. We're having a girl's night in, and we're doing manicures. Have fun with your little tykes. Love from Katie, and oh, this is Winnie, her bestest friend." She tapped the phone and smiled, plainly pleased with herself.

"If my fingernails were free—"

"Well, I'm glad they're not. You know I always look out for you. Now Jeffie knows I love you, and you love him, and it's all right for him to be out with his little friends. What makes a man happier than that? See? I might not be married, but I know what makes a man happy. They want everything. Even the sweet ones." Winnie lifted Katie's hand from the remover, and she inspected her nails critically. "They pass. Now for polish."

Katie leaned her head back and closed her eyes, letting her friend have full reign for the moment. However, she had a list, and a manicure wasn't on it. Not even in the vicinity. Ooh, Winnie, she thought. If you knew what I was thinking, you'd think me a bad, bad girl.

That made her giggle, in spite of it all, and when Winnie slapped the top of her hand and told her to hold still, she began to laugh. A girl's night in. Instead, it was Winnie's time to play dress up, even if there was a wedding two weeks away, and the list of things left undone was longer than her arm.

At least she had one thing marked off. The dresses. Just what she would see on her special day, she didn't know, but that was the fun of having Winnie for a friend. What you got was what you got, take it or leave it, and Katie knew she'd take it, no matter what her friend handed out.

Even if it was Oscar de la Renta, one of the priciest in his field.

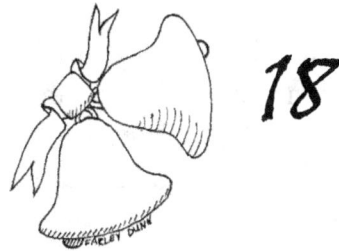

18

"This is the heaviest one yet." Katie held the moving box in two hands as she carried it to set it on top of the three boxes already taped shut and ready to ship to her new home. It was unsealed, and newspaper-wrapped items filled the inside.

It was a full week since her final day at work, a week of sorting through the personal items she brought home from her office and the small parting gifts received from her coworkers. An outsized potted flower graced the balcony, one that she'd lugged home with some difficulty. Managing her unexpected bonanza had eaten into packing her apartment. She'd appealed to Winnie full time to help her, claiming desperation. It was an honest plea, too. She still wasn't finished, and she was scheduled to be gone the following day.

"Oh, no, Sweetie. Mine was heavier." Winnie

smiled from across the room, but from the sound of her voice, her enthusiasm for packing was worn thin. She had a bandana tied around her hair, and her white jeans and lemon-colored tee were streaked with dirt. She had cotton gloves on her hands. A fresh manicure, she'd proudly boasted, as she'd pulled on the gloves to protect it.

"Wait till we get to the decorative items." Katie looked at her friend and smiled, holding up the tape. "Get this box sealed, and another one bites the dust."

She attached the tape on one side, and pressing the flaps down, with a ripping whack, she yanked tape across the top and down the other side. Once there, she cut the tape and pressed it firmly down with her fingers.

"Oh, Katie, how many left?" Winnie dropped into a chair, putting her wrist on her forehead. "You bought so many boxes. I'm certain I'm coming down with exhaustion, and it doesn't look like we've done anything in here."

"There's barely another fifteen still leaning against the wall in the entry. You're coming down with laziness, in my opinion. And no, we haven't done anything in here. All we've packed is my personal items."

"I get it." Winnie blew out a strong breath, puffing her cheeks out. "I'm your slave for the day. I'm only half African, don't you forget. You can't make me work all the time. See, I can joke even when I'm on the brink of total collapse."

"When does the work half start?"

"How about I kitchen us up a good meal?" Winnie

had one of her gloves off, inspecting her nails. "At least these are still beautiful."

"How do you kitchen up a meal?" Katie had pulled another box from the stack, and she popped it open, folding the interlocking bottom down to keep the sides from closing back up. She flipped it upside down, and with a ripping sound, she applied tape to the seam.

"With these." Winnie held up her car keys, and she jangled them. "You can go, too."

"Oh, Winnie, Winnie, Winnie! I wish I could." Katie set the tape on top of the empty box, and she fell onto the sofa. In reality, she had about done all she wanted for the day, also. "How will I get this done? A week, I thought. I had a whole week, and I haven't wasted a minute of it. Not a minute, and I'm not packed, yet. It's Friday, and I'm leaving for the island tomorrow."

Winnie was smiling broadly.

"What? If you're making fun of me, you can go to lunch and not come back. No, forget that. You have to help me pack. Oh, what is it?"

"You said you haven't wasted a minute of your week, and I've been here all the time. How sweet of you!"

"How's that a compliment?"

"You spent time with me, and not a minute of it was wasted. I'm getting you a cheesecake shake from the place with the drive-through. Do you want raspberry or vanilla?"

"Raspberry, if you must, but something real before I tackle a shake. How about a chimichanga? I like

Montecristo on Huntington. I have some money in my purse." Katie pointed to it.

"I've got it, Sweetie. Be back in a couple hours." Winnie pulled a credit card from her back pants pocket and waved it. "My treat."

"Hours? What do you mean you'll be gone hours? Is this your way of bailing on me?" Just that one word, and Katie felt overwhelmed with desperation. With Winnie here, she pictured getting finished. Alone? All she hadn't managed to get done felt like it was about to crash down on her day.

"Sweetie, it's you who wants Huntington. Do you know what the traffic's like today? It's Friday." Winnie smiled and tapped Katie on the end of the nose. She pointed around the room. "And don't you worry about all this. Everything will work out fine. I love you, God loves you, and Jeffie loves you. What more could you want?"

"Oh, you!" Winnie was right, though, and Katie felt her mood lift. She stood and saw her friend out the door, but as she closed it, the collapsed boxes beside the door reminded her accusingly that in spite of Winnie's confident assurances, only about a fourth of her possessions were boxed and ready to go. The rest . . .

She hit her forehead with the heel of her hand. Wrapping paper. Tissue paper, she meant. She had used the last that morning, substituting her used newspapers, but even those were gone. She should have given Winnie money to pick up some.

Before she could get to her phone to call her and tell her, it began to sing a bright and cheerful tune.

When she picked it up, it surprised her that it wasn't Jeff or Winnie. Or any of her friends from work. They might call, as the majority of them were heading to the island in a week to serve as members of the wedding party. No, this was just a number, with no name attached. And that was very odd.

Katie tapped the icon to answer and placed it to her ear. "Katie Carver here. How may I help you?" She cringed at the formality, but after so many years at ALDMass, she guessed it was inevitable.

"My little Katie, dear. How wonderful it is to hear your voice! I should wish to come to see you once again."

Katie recognized the voice, and she felt her day go flat. How could she have forgotten? She was to have reserved a hotel suite for her French relation, one that she understood was to be top-of-the-line. The best.

"Cousin Nikki?" Katie's mind raced on how to rectify her mistake.

"Oui, my dear. You are home, non?"

"Yes, absolutely, Cousin Nikki. Where are you?" Katie brightened her voice. She didn't dare let her dismay bleed over the line. How, though, had this very important duty gotten away from her? She was horrified—and at a total loss as to what she could do. She pictured the better hotels, first latching on Buckminster. No, better, the Boston Harbor or the Ritz-Carlton. The Four Seasons had the best suites, though. Give me twenty minutes, Nikki, she pleaded silently.

"I am here, my dear. May you give me your permission? I will also require a espace de stationnement,

s'il vous plait. Non, non, is not right. A place de parking. Non, a parking spot. Place, a parking place. I am
so sorry, my dear. Is not used to English for a long
time."

"Parking? Here?" Nikki's voice was coming across
very warmly over the phone, but she seemed to be
stuck on this. A suspicion began to nag Katie, and she
walked to the window and peered down. Dismay
pulled the light from the sky and the energy from her
limbs. Far below was the longest white limousine she
thought she'd ever seen.

"Oui, my dear. A few things I have that will not fit,
I think, in my rooms. Are you *full up*?" That was said
with a laugh.

Sure enough, the driver, in full livery, had several
large suitcases and one trunk already on the sidewalk,
and he was using a small dolly to move them into a
central pile. One of the car doors was open, and an el-
egantly dressed woman partially emerged. She wore a
smart suit in light gray; with fur around the hem, the
cuffs just at her wrists, and edging her lapels. Light
flashed from her fingers, and there was no question
what that signified. Diamonds, beyond doubt, and lots
of them by the winking glimmers of miniature suns.

The broad-brimmed hat disguised her face as the
driver stepped to her and offered his hand, helping the
stylishly attired woman to her feet. It was when he
reached back in the car and brought out a walker,
opened it and placed it in front of her, that Katie saw
deeper into her cousin. Twenty years had passed, and
while Katie had grown up, her cousin had grown old.

Nicolette looked up, showing her face, and she peered across the facade of the building. Katie just caught sight of what she thought was a Bluetooth ear-piece, when her phone spoke to her once again.

"My dear, now is a good time. We cannot block the street for always, now can we?" She waved her hand in the air, at who it was impossible to tell.

"Oh, I'm sorry, Cousin Nikki. Of course. I'll buzz you in."

"Merci, my dear. And then, s'il vous plait, we will find our way to our American residence for our extended stay in your country."

Katie's heart pounded as she hung up. She had about fifteen minutes to find a room for her cousin. Good heavens, how was she going to get this done? Her life was falling apart around her, and she was getting married in a week.

It hit her in a whole new light. One week. What had she been thinking? She had to call Jeff and have him postpone. She could not do this in one week.

It didn't help when she called the numbers to the hotels. She found fifteen minutes were fully adequate to resolve the question of a place for Nicolette to stay. However, the news wasn't exactly what she wanted to share with her cousin. They were booked solid. Why? Of course, of course! Oktoberfest. There were 200,000 attendees expected this year, and Harvard Square would be packed. This weekend had been booked for months, and no, there were no extra rooms at any price.

Before Katie could sink any further into her

mounting despair, the doorbell rang. Oh, oh, Cousin Nikki, she thought. You are going to be so disappointed in me.

With lead in her feet, Katie forced herself to the door, and brightening her face as much as she could, she pulled it wide, calling out the most energetic greeting she could manage.

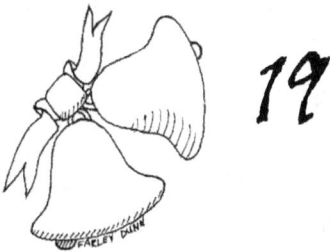

19

"Cousin Nikki!" Katie kept her voice bright in an attempt to hide the dismay that had swallowed her inside.

"Ah, ma chère!" Nicolette held out her arms, and her driver moved the walker out of the way adroitly and unobtrusively. "You, my love, so very beautiful you are. How I miss my own chance at love. Ah, tomber amoureux. To fall in love. It makes one so belle, so beautiful. Give Nikki a kiss."

In that request, Katie remembered that long-ago visit on Rockhaven, the expected kiss, and the exotic way her cousin had conversed half in French and half in English. It also seemed by the end of the visit, the French had transformed itself into full conversations in understandable words. She hoped this would be the same, or she'd be forever trying to figure out what her cousin wanted to say.

At the moment, though, her words had been pretty clear. She expected a kiss, and if Katie remembered correctly, it was more a brushing of cheek to cheek, rather than a true kiss.

Katie smiled broadly and replied, "Of course. Welcome to my home and to America." She stepped forward, and gently touching Nikki's arms, she brought her face next to her cousin's and made a soft kissing sound.

"Comme c'est beau! A wonderful flat. Charming, I believe you must say here in America. Now, the view. Show me." Nicolette wrapped one of Katie's arms in hers and moved into the apartment, rather better than her walker suggested she might.

"Absolutely." Katie glanced into the hallway to see the driver standing against the wall just beside the door, his hands behind his back. At his side was the set of cases Katie had seen on the sidewalk below. Now, she wondered, what's that all about? Out loud, she spoke to her guest. "This way. I have a small balcony you can enjoy the breeze from."

"From which, my dear. But, ah! You young people. You do not use so much the prepositions in the way to which I am familiar. Forgive an old woman." Nicolette tapped her forehead with her fingertips and smiled. "Show me this small balcony of yours."

The breezes were fresh, but they were also a little much for the elderly woman, she declared after a short time of viewing the different landmarks. Once inside, she removed her hat, and offering it to Katie—who had no idea what to do with it except place it on her bed—she seated herself on the sofa.

"You are leaving, are you not, on the morrow?" Nicolette's eyes had roamed the room, and now she looked directly at Katie. She seemed amused, for whatever reason.

"Oh, you saw my boxes." Katie was reminded in that question of all she hadn't completed. Her list! It wasn't getting marked off, and she squelched the panic that tried to rear its head once again. "I have a friend who's been helping me, but she's off on an errand."

"Ah. Je la connais." Nicolette tapped her forehead once again. "My apologies. I forget I am no longer in France. I should say, I know her. Winnie, am I correct?" She smiled as if the answer were obvious.

"Yes!" Katie was surprised her cousin knew her friend's name. "You can't have met before, I don't think. She's just been in the Caribbean, but France?" Katie shrugged.

"Elle est au téléphone." Nicolette waved one hand dismissively in the air. "I call here one day, and your Winnie speak with me. She is a very charming girl."

"Oh, yes." Katie raised her eyebrows at that. "Very charming, I am sure. She's my bridesmaid." She said that brightly.

"Yes, yes. For next week, it is such a wonderful thing to have a dependable bridesmaid. For now, though, when is the compagnie de déménagement arriving to vacate your flat? Surely you must be ready at that time!" Nicolette smiled as if this was a pertinent detail, and she was making very relevant observations.

"Compagnie de déménagement. Um, management company? I'm not sure what you mean."

"Um, l'instigateur, non. Um, locomotive. To marche." Nicolette frowned at her choice of words.

"Moving? Moving company!" Katie grinned. "Oh, there is no moving company. Jeff, that's my fiancé, he has a houseful of furniture. I have no room for this. My friend Winnie is selling it all for me."

"Vendant? You will sell all of this? Why do you not keep your flat, if you must sell your fine things?" Nicolette used the arm of the sofa to stand, and she walked to the kitchen, using tabletops and walls along the way to steady herself. "My little Katie, this is quite nice. You have, shall we say, taste in the most exquisite manner."

"Money," Katie called as she followed her cousin, pleased to see she was really quite capable on her own. "You do know Grandmamma's story, I suppose."

"Of course, dear Katie. It is so very sad."

"I've held a job, and it paid for this, but I'm off to Maine. Tomorrow, as you know." Her cousin's words tweaked Katie's emotions, however. She had thought the very same thing, which was why her personal items had been the first to be boxed, and she'd left the rest of the apartment untouched for as long as possible.

"If you sell quickly, will you regain your money?" Before Katie could come up with a reply, Nicolette had opened a drawer, and she lovingly stroked Katie's flatware. "This, dear, you cannot know, but it is the same as my grandmamma's."

"It's similar to my grandmother's, too. I guess

that's why I chose it." Katie reached in and took a spoon. She rubbed her thumb across the ornate pattern in the handle before replacing it. "I like that your grandmother had something similar. It makes it a family pattern, in a way."

"You have the original, still?" Nicolette pursed her lips, as she pulled her hand from the drawer and gently closed it.

"Grandmamma's?" Katie smiled, and she looked through the dining room to the view outside the windows. "If it was in the house up on Carver Point, it was lost. I'm sorry, no."

Katie turned to her cousin to see her eyes red rimmed, and she seemed diminished.

"I hoped always to see it again. When I see these, my heart soars. Now I know they are gone." Then, Nicolette straightened her back, and she said more forcefully, "You are leaving tomorrow, am I still correct?"

"I have ferry reservations at 2:45."

"Your grandmamma's house. It has been rebuilt, non?" Nicolette began making her way to the dining room window. There, she paused, taking in the view from both directions. One hand rested on the tabletop for support.

"Non." Katie smiled at using the French for no.

"Where do you stay?" Nicolette seemed surprised at Katie's response.

"Do you remember the sleeping cabin out on the Point?"

"Oui. By the water, is correct?"

"There. My fiancé put in a generator, and that's

141

where I'll be over the next week."

"Ah, let me think." Nicolette's pointer finger tapped. "This flat, it is one bedroom, I think. Only one?"

"Yes, although it has a loft. There's a bed up there, but I don't think you could make the climb."

"Francois is the one who will be there. Do you own the flat, or is leased year to year?"

"Month to month. Well, year to year, but I pay month to month."

"Forgive me for asking, my dear, but a decision now arises. I must have information. Let me ask bluntly. The lease, it is terminated, non?"

Katie laughed in an embarrassed way. That was something that bothered her. She knew she was moving, but she hadn't told the management yet. With her furniture unsold, what could she do? Winnie had promised to stay here until all the major pieces were gone, and the rest they would donate to charity, if Jeff couldn't find a place for them on the island.

"I see. You have not yet returned the lease." Nicolette gently took Katie's hand, and she squeezed it, smiling. "Then we must make arrangements. C'est plus facile à dire qu'à faire to find good lodgings, and I will help you in this." She nodded her head in a brief bob, as if that settled the entire matter.

"What did you just say? Just now in French, I mean?" Katie wasn't sure she was on the same page as her cousin, but then the older woman operated in a different world, culturally and financially.

"C'est plus facile à dire qu'à faire? I am so sorry. I

should speak English full time. It means," and she paused, searching, "when something is hard to do, but easy to say."

"Easier said than done." Katie smiled.

"Oui. Very exact."

"So, what are we doing?"

"Ah, we are making a plan. Cancel all my réservations. I will stay here, for as long as you will let me." Nicolette's eyes twinkled impishly. "And I think that may be a long time, as I think you are very in love."

"You want to rent my apartment?"

"Oui, little Katie. It is perfect, is it not? All your fine things. Grandmamma's silver, it will all be here for you to use again."

"Are you sure? And it's not really my grandmother's silver."

"Oh, dear, I am aware. It is the memory I am enjoying. And oui, it is what I am sure of. Francois, upstairs he will sleep, and he is mine always. He will be shopping boy and service ménager. Housekeeper, I intend to say. Leave what you will, and it will be here when you return." Nicolette's pronouncement was matter-of-fact, and she looked around the room, her eyes not missing one detail.

"Rent is still due, Nikki." Katie hoped she didn't think she could live here for free. Katie had saved back enough for a month or two, but that was being reimbursed by the sale of her furniture, she hoped.

"Oui. Is less than one night for Francois and myself at a good établissement. I will have a home in America, and all with saving much expense. Who can

143

ask for better than this? It will be no problem to cancel, oui?"

"Your hotel reservations?" Katie smiled, feeling the tension from earlier melt away. It would be the easiest thing in the world, especially as she'd never made them in the first place. "For you, Cousin Nikki, it will be no problem at all."

"Now for parking for the car. It is very big. How shall we park a very big car in your American city?" Nicolette smiled with that impish look in her eyes. "Perhaps we must find a smaller car?"

"Just not too small, Cousin. That's a lot of luggage out in the hall."

"Non, ma chère." Nicolette looked surprised. "Is not much at all. Is reason for very big car. Is full, how shall we say, to the brim." She laughed at that. "For a very long stay, Cousin Nikki needs all the things that make her happy."

"I expect you will be very happy during your stay, then."

"Now, about this man of yours. When I was young like you, the men to me were as butterflies to a beautiful flower . . ."

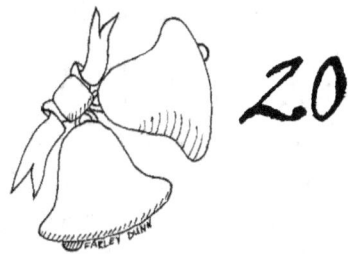

20

"Don't say anything. I have a full explanation." Katie held her hand up to silence Winnie's look at the cases piled along one wall in her living room.

"But, Sweetie, we were packing." Winnie's sunglasses were in her hair, an extra set of eyes just over her forehead, and in one hand she held a plastic sack with Montecristo artfully written on the side. From her other hand dangled her keys, and they jangled with the swinging of her hand as she spoke. "Do we have to move the stuff from this to those?"

Her eyes looked from the four taped boxes to the pile of Nicolette's cases.

"I do have an explanation. I was about to explain." Katie took a deep breath.

"No, no. I get it. I'm gone for one minute, and you have a change of plans. Well, tell me, Sweetie, how

145

you managed to afford these. I know good luggage, and this is the best." She had set the sack on the taped boxes, and with one fingertip, she traced an intertwined Y and S and L on the outside of the closest case. "If you can afford this, you can afford to *give* me all this stuff. Why bother moving anything? Just buy more." Winnie dropped onto the sofa, and she crossed her arms and looked away.

"Okay, I get it. You're irritated. What?" Katie sat on the coffee table, and she took Winnie's hands in hers. "It can't be just this luggage. Now, give."

"On the island." She sniffled, pulling one hand loose and brushing at her eyes. "I used an outdoor potty all week, and you had money to put in a real bathroom."

"Oh, so that's it." Katie laughed, and slapping her hands to her knees, she stood, motioning to the cases. "These aren't mine. Cousin Nikki, the one you didn't tell me you talked to? She was here, and this is all hers."

"Oh." Winnie bit at one finger. "One little-bitty detail I forgot. I gave her your address, and she's coming today. There. I told you. Are we okay, now?"

"Well, you don't have to sell any of my stuff, anymore." Katie smirked. "It's already taken care of."

"Katie! I wanted your sofa. How could you sell it already? I just needed to get the price down." Winnie stood and huffed, then she walked to pull the sack roughly off the boxes and take it to the kitchen. "I'm hungry. I bought me a chimichanga, too. Here's yours if you still want it." She pulled the second one out and plopped it heavily on the counter.

"Honey!" Katie went to her. "You never told me you wanted the sofa. When Cousin Nikki moves out, you can still have it."

"Oh!" Winnie wailed. "Now she's living here, too? Did you give her everything? I wanted to buy your lamp, too."

"Okay, enough spoiled baby. Now you listen like I asked you to when you first came in. My cousin is here from France, my very wealthy cousin is here from France, and she wants to stay for an extended time. I forgot to reserve her a hotel suite, and now she's staying here. It's like a sublet."

Winnie looked at her with a twinkle in her eyes, and she was trying to fight a smile.

"Get it out. What have I said now?"

"You forgot to get your cousin a hotel room, during Oktoberfest? Oh, that's funny. What did your cousin say?" She giggled, her sandwich forgotten for the moment.

"She doesn't know, and shush, you don't need to tell her. She saw my flatware, and she decided she'd rather stay here than at a hotel. I lucked out."

"Your flatware, hm-m." Winnie opened the drawer and pulled out a knife. "I mean, it's nice enough, but I don't know that I'd rent an apartment just for the flatware."

"That shows what you know." Katie took the knife and dropped it back into the drawer. "It resembles my grandmother's from the island, which I didn't know was Cousin Nikki's grandmother's set from France."

"Who has your grandmother's set now?" Winnie had the drawer back open just a bit to where the ends of the flatware showed.

"You were there." Katie had the chimichanga in her hand by then, and she pulled a plate from the cabinet. The food had cooled and needed a minute in the microwave. She pushed Winnie aside and slipped it in, hitting the Quick Cook twice for one minute total time. She looked back at Winnie expectantly. "So?"

"Okay. There wasn't anything there. I guess it was burned up or sold." She had her sandwich on a plate, and she waited for the oven.

"Sold?" Katie was growing impatient, either that or very hungry. Sold? Hadn't she seen the empty basement? Everything was gone.

"Okay, burned. Nothing was left. I remember you telling me that. I just thought, nothing was left, but what wasn't there had maybe been sold. Some things sometimes are found after a fire. Metal. Fire. Metal things should be okay." She made a face like, duh.

"Well, it wasn't, and I bought this just for the memory. Now with Nikki here, we're finished packing. Want to return some unused boxes with me?"

"Finished? Sweetie, that's the best news I've heard all week. If I packed one more box, I'd be too tired to get in the spa, and I'm never too tired to get in the spa."

They were at the table with their food by then, and for a moment, the silence of the very hungry reigned. Shakes followed, which Katie had to admit were very good, as they tasted each other's, and found them equally satisfying.

As they were finishing, Winnie's attention was drawn back to the luggage filling half the room.

"Did your cousin hire a moving truck? This is a lot of stuff."

"A moving car. A limousine, to be exact." Katie gathered up the paper, and she dropped it in the trash bin under the sink. "They've gone to get a smaller one, one that'll fit in the parking garage."

"They? I thought this was just your cousin."

"And Francois." Katie looked expectantly at her friend, letting her stew on that word.

"Francois? Like, male friend?" Her expression brightened with interest. "I think I like your cousin Nikki, and I haven't yet met her."

"Oh, I give in. He's her chauffeur." Katie sat at the table, letting herself be caught up in the excitement of it all. This had been her grandmother's world, although Katie remembered very little of it. Her grandmamma had always had caretakers at the Maine property, people who put the boats out every year and placed them back in storage in the fall. And in winter in the city, a driver, but it wasn't something Katie had really paid attention to. It had just been Grandmamma, and it was in the summer when Katie spent time with her. On the island, there had been no drivers at all, just the occasional delivery service showing up at the dock or down the drive, as normal as the summer day was long on a Maine island fifteen miles out to sea.

"Your cousin has a chauffeur." Winnie breathed in deeply, an enraptured expression on her face.

"And he does housecleaning, laundry, and grocery shopping. But sure, she has a chauffeur."

"And I could ride in her limousine."

"No, you can't." Katie tried not to laugh. "You missed it. They've gone to get a smaller car. Remember what I said? The big one wouldn't fit in the garage."

"Oh." Winnie shrugged. Then she said, more excitedly, "Oh! Francois can take you to the airport tomorrow. Can I ride along?"

"Sure, Honey, sure." Katie laughed, and gave her a hug. "But I'm driving my car. I'm not flying up."

"Then," Winnie still held on, whispering in Katie's ear, "Can I use him on Sunday?"

"Sunday? To church?" Katie pushed her away.

"Uh! Don't you ever listen? I have a cowboy shoot. They're flying me to Colorado Sunday afternoon." Winnie huffed. "I have to go to the airport sometimes, too, and you won't be here, now."

"You're going to Colorado just like that." Katie shook her head in dismay. How come her friend always took off when Katie needed her most? "And did you tell them your best friend's getting married next week?"

"I wouldn't let 'em forget. My return ticket is to Maine." Winnie giggled. "It's like a free trip up there. And because I'm flying out of Logan, they gave me another voucher from Maine back to here."

"Oh, you bad girl." Katie teased, but she was glad to have this news. If her friend already had her flight scheduled, she might even make it. There was one more question she had to ask. "The dresses—"

She got cut off, though.

"No, don't even ask. I'll have them there when I show up, and not a minute before. Anyway, you know it's bad luck to have the groom see the bride in the dress before she walks the aisle. I don't trust you, so I'm keeping the dress."

"Dresses." Katie wanted that clear, as it seemed to her Winnie had taken them over.

"Dresses. I have them all, and I'll have them there, and I don't want another word said."

Two voices came drifting through the open front door, both speaking fluently in French. One was Cousin Nikki, and they both recognized that one. The second got a frown from Winnie.

"Sweetie, you did say your cousin's chauffeur is named Francois. He. That is a man's name, right?"

Katie smiled. She knew who the other voice belonged to. Her cousin had found Miss Annie from Trinity. Katie was glad. They'd be good company for each other while Cousin Nikki was here.

A man's voice joined the first two. He also spoke in French.

"Oh, thank goodness," Winnie said, with a laugh. "For a minute, I thought that . . . um . . . ."

"You thought what?" Katie teased. She could see her friend's face flush. It was hard to pick up on with her beautiful and perpetually tanned complexion, but she was definitely blushing.

"Just that, oh, that Francois . . ." and without finishing her statement, she stood and walked toward the door, calling out, "Welcome to Boston, Cousin Nikki. I'm Winnie, the one you spoke with on the phone—"

Katie sat back and laughed. Winnie was Winnie, and that was all there was to it. She felt better, though. With Nikki's arrival, she'd been able to strike about ten things off her list, from utilities to furniture to who was going to collect her mail. She could even wait until after the ceremony and honeymoon to get to the post office and update her address.

It seemed the storms of change were clearing, and maybe she and Jeff could merge their lives on time after all.

The one thing she couldn't put off this afternoon was to call Janine. If the cabin wasn't ready, she'd have no place to stay. Then there was gasoline for the generator, clean linens, and the drive. She had to have someone to check to see if it was still passable. It had been July when she was last out, and it was now the end of September. No one was going to have a sailboat out there, and few people left their docks out after the middle of the month. It was the drive or nothing.

Katie slipped a sheet of paper from her binder, and she began to scribble. She'd just thought the list was getting shorter. Now it was longer than ever.

What, oh what would she do? Winnie could handle some of these, she decided. Then she remembered Winnie's run for lunch. Her cousin's words came back to her. C'est plus facile à dire qu'à faire. She remembered exactly what it meant. Getting help from Winnie would be easier said than done.

Katie leaned forward and wrote one more thing on

152

her list. *Thank Winnie for being the best friend ever.* Then, with her pen, she circled it three times. If she didn't get any of the others done, that one she would make sure of. She knew now it was the most important item of all.

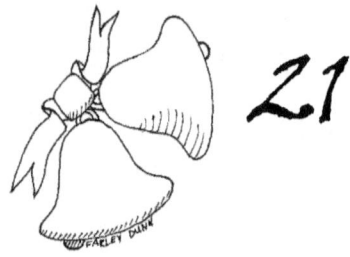

21

It was the smell of salt and spruce, and the tang of diesel fuel that told Katie she was almost home.

On the drive up I-95, rain had drizzled and spit on her windshield. Yet, once the ferry had broken free of the harbor, and fifteen miles of ocean had stretched in front of her, the clouds had given way to shards of broken sunlight, then gradually evaporated altogether.

Now, seabirds danced across the waves, and the clang of sea buoys drew Katie in. She had always loved the sound of the buoys as they warned seafarers that there was danger if one came too close. Finally, they were hers forever, if she could pull off a wedding in a week's time.

Off in the distance was the misty profile of the up-coming island, and she looked for the spruce-topped finger that ended in Carver Point. She could also catch

Spurgeon Light standing tall in the sea if she kept her eyes on just the right spot. It was easy to miss, and she refused to let herself get distracted.

Distracted. She smiled at that. Everything about her wedding had kept her distracted. If she wished for anything, it would be someone to take the planning from her and let her just enjoy this special time. A mother, maybe, and a father. She let herself dream of that for a moment. This week would indeed be easier if she had a mother to plan all this for her, and a father to pay for it. But, that was not her case. They were gone, and if she wanted it to happen, it was up to her.

She closed her eyes to the breeze and turned her face to the sun, smiling. She had her faith in God, her good friend Winnie, and Jeff waiting for her on Rockhaven. That was what counted. The Carver fortune that had once allowed her family to live well? Katie had never shared in it, only unknowingly enjoying the final days of its demise, never realizing that her family had once had money that was mostly gone by the time she'd arrived. What a wedding she could have planned if the Carver riches were still around!

If wishes were fishes. Katie opened her eyes and laughed. The Carver estate had burned a decade and a half before, the money was gone, and she had learned to live with that. Besides, she and Jeff would be living in his house just outside of town. The Point was inaccessible during winter. Snow, fallen trees, it didn't matter. The Point was for summer. Town was for winter. Even if Carver House still graced the rocky promontory on Carver Point, it wouldn't have made a full-time residence.

Now, the islands surrounded her, as the ferry pulled between Settler's Island and Rockhaven. It was as beautiful every time she returned as it was the first visit each summer.

The ferry was mostly empty, with the deceptive weather on the mainland and the lateness of the season, but a family with two small children stood at the front of the boat with Katie, oohing and aahing as each new exposed ledge and island came into view. This close to Rockhaven, a thin layer of fog still hovered just above the level of the sea, reaching like tenuous fingers to wrap the shore in otherworldly vapors. Tree-covered rocky outcrops and undersea ledges breaking through the waves grew out of the mist, washed out and vague at first, then finally coming in plain view to delight the children.

The little girl called, "There! Daddy! What's that?" and she pointed to a dark object floating in the water.

Katie knew before the man answered, and she took this as a sign from God. An answered prayer, even if it wasn't one she'd specifically prayed. What had she told Jeff back in July? There should be seals. There should always be seals at Rockhaven. Of course, the one that had sunned itself on her little beach out on the Point hadn't exactly charmed Winnie, but still. There should always be seals.

"It's a spotted seal, honey." The father squatted behind his daughter, wrapping her in one arm, and pointing with the other. "See? It has spots on it."

"Does it like swimming?" The little girl's voice

was high-pitched and clear.

"Probably." Her father called to the brother. "Levi, come see this. Your sister found a seal. I told you I used to see seals out here growing up."

Katie stepped away, leaving the family to their discoveries. She envied those children. Her own parents hadn't loved the island and had rarely come out. Her children, should she have any, would get the chance to love this place just as much as Katie did. More, even, because they would live here.

The ferry broached the last outcropping, and Rockhaven Harbor came into view, with its boats tied to their moorings and all the houses along the shore, many with brightly painted doors and shutters, and others wrapped in their wooden shingle cocoons.

Many of the pleasure boats were gone, and that was nice. Katie hadn't thought of that. Late September brought the end to the season, and the summer people wouldn't return for another eight months. It felt odd saying that. Summer people. She had been one of those, only here for the best months of the year. Now she would have to rethink herself, becoming an islander.

In any case, the harbor free of summer yachts was a nice surprise, and she let the revelation be her own private moment of enjoyment, sort of icing on her cake. Her wedding cake, if she had her way.

At the change in the sound of the engines as the boat slowed to approach the terminal, Katie climbed in her car and rolled a window down, preparing to pull onto the island in a brand-new way. In spite of her cousin's assurances that she need take nothing with her, the little car was filled completely. The four boxes? Check. Her favorite plant? Check. Food for her week on the Point? Check. Then there were all the little things she had grabbed at the last moment, thinking, how can I leave this behind? Half the stuff? Probably useless, and she would wish she'd left it. If she'd left it, she'd wish she'd brought it, so here it was.

Her stomach fluttered with butterflies. Jeff would be waiting, his hand offering her a life she'd always wanted and now could see just hundreds of feet away. She wasn't sure if her butterflies were anticipation or a warning, but decisions had been made, and her life was changing.

The ferry shifted roughly, and it was at the terminal. Just in front of Katie, a woman in an orange bib flipped a lever on a post, and the ramp dropped to mate with the front of the ferry. She started the engine, and with some difficulty—the car was very packed—she pulled the lever to release the parking brake. At a signal from the orange-trimmed woman, Katie shifted into gear and pulled forward into her brand-new life.

"Janine!" Katie waved through her window. Her friend had one of her sons in tow, one of the smaller two. Her hand firmly grasped the collar of the boy's sweater. Jeff was nowhere to be seen, and Katie felt a moment of deflation. She called to her, "Let me find a spot."

"There's one right up here." Janine pointed to one Katie hadn't seen, waving her forward. "Jeff stepped away for a minute."

"Jeff's here? Good!" A thrill of anticipation surged through her, lifting Katie's spirits. Jeff had indeed come to meet her! She glanced around. "Where?"

"There!" It was the boy, and he pointed before jerking free from his mother's hand, and running toward Jeff. He crashed into him with both fists up and balled into weapons. "Where's my candy?"

"Whoa!" Jeff held a small bag high over his head. "Not so fast, Karl."

"My name's Karlton. Karl's for babies. Give it to me!" He jumped for the hand.

"Not when you're like this. Hi, Katie!" Jeff called to her, waving with the hand holding the package. The other was on the boy's head, keeping him from jumping. With a laugh, he wrapped his arm around the boy, holding him tightly against his side. "Go park, and we'll wait."

Katie pulled in and shut off the car, her heart pounding. That boy! Still, this was Janine, and she had come to greet her. In any case, Jeff seemed to have him under control, even if he was determined to be a crazy little devil. Katie pictured the Saturday morning cartoon character based on the Tasmanian devil, no more than a black whirlwind across the television screen. It was enough to make one swear off children forever.

"A hug?" Jeff called to her from behind her car.

"Coming!" She opened the door and climbed out.

"You get my right side." Jeff's eyes twinkled. "I've got my other favorite person on my left." He pulled the boy tighter before releasing him just a bit, leaning down slightly to whisper to him not very softly, "And if you kick, no chocolate at all. I'll eat every bite."

"Mom!" The boy yelled it out.

"You've got your hands full." Katie took his empty arm and folded herself into it. She leaned to give him a kiss on the side of his mouth.

"Now I've got my hands full. I don't mind, as long as one of my arms is around you." He kissed her on her temple.

"You are so silly. I've got a carload, and I need to get to the cabin. How are the plans coming along?" Wedding plans, she knew he'd understand.

"Shush!" He nodded to the terminal building, where Janine was just coming out the door. She had disappeared inside once Jeff had taken control of her son. "Mostly okay, I think, but the rest? I'll let you discuss it with Janine." He shrugged.

"What's not okay?" That didn't sound good to Katie.

"Mom!" Karlton yelled again. "Jeff's telling."

"You little rat." Jeff handed Katie the package, and laughing, he picked the boy up in both hands, one arm under his back, and the other under his legs, and began walking toward the street. "You may not get another candy bar until you're eighteen."

"Sorry. Restroom break. What's that about?" Janine stepped up beside her, pointing at the boy and the man, now already to the sidewalk. Karlton was waving his arms and kicking his feet, but Jeff clearly had him under control, and he wasn't getting free.

"I don't know." Katie waved the scene off with a brush of her hand. "You, though, how've you and Al been holding up?"

"You mean with Daddy?" At Katie's nod, she continued, "The boys keep us so busy we haven't had time to really grieve. You know how they are. But let's not talk about that. Your wedding. I'm so excited. It's next

161

week."

"Everything's falling in place?" Katie had been on the phone with requests and reminders, but Janine had told her repeatedly that it was all taken care of. Not to worry, Katie. Not to worry. Everything'll be ready.

Well, now, after Jeff's remark, then the boy's response, she wasn't so sure.

"I see your car's full." Janine peered into the windows. "Mine's back in town. Jeff thought Karlie needed to burn off some energy. Do you want to walk in with me, or take this out now? I can bring you back to your car."

"How's the cabin?" Was it ready, she asked. She'd just called yesterday, and on such short notice, she could only hope.

"Okay, I think. I sent Tammie Barker's girl out. You don't know Tammie, but her daughter said she could use the work with fall coming on. Al's been swamped with the boat, now that he's got his cast off. Everything's piled up with him not able to go out properly. Kevie went out a few times to pull traps, but finally Al said it was more work with the boy than alone." Janine barked a laugh and shook her head.

"What's that about?" However, Katie could imagine.

"I could have told him that eleven years ago." Janine smiled. "Town or to your place? Either's okay with me. I just need to get together with you in the next day to sort out wedding details."

"I've got food in the car, and a plant. I really need to unload. I'll try Jeff on the phone, but if I can't get him, let him know I'll be back in town today. All I'm doing is unloading. You're wonderful, Janine. I couldn't do any of this without you." Katie gave her friend a warm hug before backing away and stepping to grasp her door handle.

"I feel the same, with Daddy and his, um, well." Janine's eyes were red, and she wiped at one. Then she brightened her expression. "You, go unload, and I'll tell Jeff you're coming back in. Oh, I have a great idea. My house tonight. It won't be fancy, but you and Jeff have to come. It's the only day something's not planned between now and the wedding. Okay?"

"I wouldn't miss it." Katie tapped her fingers to her lips and blew Janine a kiss. Then she dropped into the car. Something had her thinking, though. Every day this week? What could possibly be planned every day this week? She had no time for that. She had a wedding to pull together, one she wasn't absolutely sure she could get done.

Starting the car and pulling out of the lot gave her time to think, though, and as she passed the pond, she laughed at herself. Why did she think everything planned on this island was all about her? There could be quilting meetings, maybe a Town Council meeting, or even a meeting of the library committee. Good heavens, it could be the week for the monthly school board meeting. Lots of things happened on the island, and most of them weren't about her.

She had a whole week, she didn't have to clear out her apartment, and Janine said she had everything concerning the wedding under control. Goodness, even her dress was taken care of. Winnie had promised, and when had her friend ever let her down, really let her down?

After all, she was on her island, and she was here to stay. Life was perfect, and there was nothing that could get in her way.

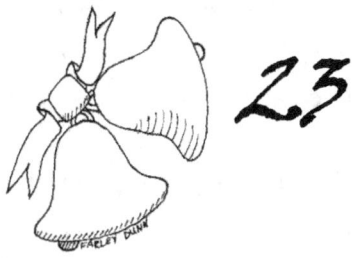

23

The September evening was only slightly cool, and as the horizon dimmed to reds and golds, the four friends sat in lawn chairs on a deck without railings. Beyond the trees, the ocean reflected the colors of the sky. Wire lobster pots filled one side of the yard, and the four boys were off chasing each other in the near darkness. Several dogs, one very large, tried to insert themselves into the action, occasionally barking at the passing bodies.

The meal may have been simple island comfort food, but it was good. Janine had fixed a big casserole of lobster mac with handmade rolls and Indian pudding afterward. Katie was stuffed.

She sat next to Jeff, and they held hands as she soaked up how wonderful life on Rockhaven could be. This was a week to be enjoyed, and she planned to make the most of it.

Janine stepped from the house, letting the screen slam behind her, and she carried four steaming mugs. "Cocoa," she whispered secretly, "for the adults."

"Thanks, Love." Al took one, and he wrapped his hands around it. He looked with creased eyebrows at Jeff. "Lots of empty pots, and best time of year."

Katie knew what he meant. He had a lot of empty pots that weren't out there catching cash to survive the upcoming winter.

"I'm here for you." Jeff took a cup from Janine, and he leaned forward, wrapping it much the same as Al. "When this week is done, we'll double up and get you up to speed."

"Right there, and I appreciate your time. Janine and I, we need some catching up after this past month. Come, let me show you something. I got this new idea for hauling pots . . ." He and Jeff had risen as he spoke, and they moved off into the dark. After a minute, lights flickered on past the lobster pots, and the men could be heard discussing something or the other that had to do with lobstering.

"Men." Janine shook her head. "That's all Al thinks about, his boat and his pots. With his arm, he's had to come up with ways to keep working. I think he thinks he's become an inventor. Something with pulleys and stuff." She laughed, but not loudly.

"You said you wanted to get with me." Katie shifted the conversation, but carefully. "What do you need from me for extra help?"

"What do I need?" Janine laughed, and it had a

166

manic edge to it. "You know, when Al and I got married, you could say we got hitched. It was less a wedding than a break in lobstering, and not a long one. He'd gotten in his first real boat, and he was about as interested in it as in me."

"I can see he loves what he does. Jeff's the same."

"You're lucky. Jeff has a real life besides his boat." Janine acted like she wanted to say more, but she took a sip of her cocoa, instead.

"So, details," Katie prompted.

"Details. Right." Janine set her cup on the deck at her feet. "Places to stay. You asked me to set up accommodations for the wedding party. I've been working on that." Again, she stopped.

"What do you have so far?" Something, Katie hoped. It was this week that she needed it.

"I haven't tied anything down just yet. People want to hold out for the best prices until they're sure the last summer people are gone. Even then, there's nothing cheap. Several of the B&Bs are closing this weekend, and the motel is booked, already. Some are your people, I assume. You have eight attendants that need a place to stay, right?"

"Plus a few others." Katie touched the heel of her hand to her forehead. "My cousin. She just arrived yesterday, and I'd forgotten. Then there's Winnie, and Connie—my supervisor at work—to put up. I expect several spouses, so, twenty, maybe twenty-four. Oh, my cousin has a chauffeur. He'll need a bed, too. What about houses? There's bound to be lots empty this late. Can we rent?"

"I'm glad you brought that up. I didn't know if you wanted to try for one big house." She paused. "It's expensive." The smallest boy ran onto the deck, and Janine called out, "Not now, Keithie. Mommy's got business."

"Mommy," he began to wail.

"Kevie! Come get your brother. Five minutes. All I asked for was five minutes." She yelled it into the dark.

"Okay, Mom. It's been longer than five minutes already." The oldest boy ran up and grabbed his brother by the shirt and dragged him off, telling him, "I told you you'd get me yelled at. You're going to wish . . ."

Katie didn't want to hear the rest. As long as all four boys were alive when she drove off, she was good with that. Janine was already going on, though, and Katie turned her attention to what she was saying.

"Briar House is empty. I've talked to Peg Briar, and she said if we'll pay cleaning before and after, she can let us have it at a good discount."

"That big Victorian, the one just in town?" Katie didn't know it rented. "I thought it was a full-time residence."

"After the captain died, the kids opened it up. It's big."

"I was in it once." Katie hadn't toured it all, but her grandmother had taken her there to pick up or deliver something. What, she didn't remember, but it had seemed dark and overflowing with heavy furniture.

"Nine bedrooms, and the attic has been opened up for more sleeping space." Janine sipped more of her cocoa, her hands now wrapped around the cup. The air was cooling fast.

"Done. Briar House it is. I suppose some people must already have houses rented for the weekend, those that aren't at the motel, anyway. We'll squeeze as many in Briar House as possible. You said, and it's Tammie, right? Tammie Baker's daughter is cleaning? Can we use her?"

The talk went on, getting the accommodations settled, and backup locations for lodgings squared away. Jeff and Al returned, sending Janine inside for more cocoa, and they pulled their chairs to the edge of the deck. One of the dogs, the big one, joined them, lying sideways against Al's chair legs, and nudging his foot until Al reached one hand to scratch behind its ears. The light was still on past the lobster pots, casting just enough of a glow that the four adults were able to see each other easily.

The boys' voices filtered in from somewhere, and once there was a loud splash. In the resulting silence, Janine made to stand, softly calling Al's name, but the boys started yelling, and Al raised one finger at a time, naming each boy. When he had all four identified, Janine relaxed back into her seat.

As the evening was wrapping up, Katie was surprised to find she was expected at an event the following evening. Al mentioned it first.

"Ah, ready for the social tomorrow?" He said it offhand, as if he assumed she knew about it.

"Social?" Katie looked to Jeff and Janine. "What social?"

"Oh," Jeff said, grimacing. "I, um, guess I thought you knew. It's something that's sort of expected for island weddings." He shrugged.

"I should have thought." They were back inside, and Janine was repackaging leftover food into smaller containers. She laughed as if it was no big deal. "Al and I had one. I forget you've not been here for a long time. It's not a dance, but imagine a big barn dance. It's in the town hall."

"And what goes on, if I may ask?" A barn dance that's not a dance?

"Dancing." Al looked at Janine, and something passed between them. Good memories, perhaps. "If I have my say about it."

"It's an island meet-and-greet. For you, a welcome to island life." Jeff took one of her hands in both of his.

"A church thing? They were at the Point in the summer."

"More." Janine stood from placing food in the fridge. "Everyone comes to this. Sometimes they bring instruments, and impromptu music starts up."

"Electric guitar." Al did an "air" guitar, and he "twanged" it, grinning. "It's fun."

"Sure." Katie smiled brightly. "I didn't know, but sure. What time?"

"Four." Janine. "You don't worry about the food, either. I've already planned what everyone's bringing, the ones who'd listen to me. Just expect lots of pies."

"Lots of pies." Jeff smiled broadly.

"Dancing," Al reminded them.

"This is the biggest thing planned for the week. Everything else? Don't worry. It'll be fun." Janine's eyes sparkled.

Everything else? Before Katie could come up with an appropriate response, the door slammed open, and in came the nine-year-old Peavey, and he was dripping wet and mad as a hornet.

"I'm going to beat up Kevie. This is the second time. Tonight." Without another word, he threw himself up the stairs, taking them two at a time, and disappeared from view.

The other three boys crashed through the door, and their eyes gleamed in excitement, calling out all at once, "Where's Konnar?" Al pointed to the stairs, and in a tumble of arms and legs, they disappeared after him.

"Until tomorrow?" Katie decided it was a good time to make her exit. Asking about the "everything else"? Maybe she didn't want to know.

"I'll see you out." Jeff stepped up and took her arm. He leaned in to whisper, "At least all the island's wild animals are upstairs."

"I heard that." Janine narrowed her eyes at him, but she fought a smile at the same time.

Something crashed upstairs, and Al and Janine took to the stairs together, leaving Katie and Jeff to let themselves out. It also gave them time to say goodnight, which, to say it nicely, needed a little private time.

A hug and a kiss. Who wanted to watch that, except three dogs that only cared about having their ears

171

scratched?

All-in-all, Katie drove home afterward thinking the evening had wrapped up pretty well. Yep, with Jeff as the dessert, it had wrapped up pretty well, indeed.

With Jeff on her mind, who cared about what was happening tomorrow night, or the next night, or the next? Only Saturday counted, because that was the day she was getting married.

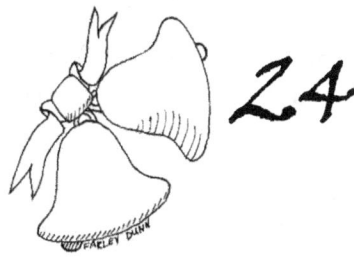

"Winnie, can I do this?"

Katie stood in front of a floor-length mirror, and her stomach churned. She wore a mid-thigh Oscar de la Renta wedding gown in white and pale blue. It was a princess dress, and she did not feel like a princess bride.

"You are beautiful, Sweetie." Winnie stood behind her and put her hands on Katie's shoulders. "Even Oscar would have to agree, no one could wear this dress any better."

Katie's week had been a whirlwind. Last Sunday's social? That had only been the start. Janine's prediction that the rest would be fun? Exhausting was the word. Monday's lingerie gala? Who knew isolated island women were aware of so many types of unusual undergarments. "What else do we have to think of all winter?" one very elderly woman had murmured to her. Tuesday? Cake testing. No wonder the island bakery came so highly recommended. Icing coated everyone's lips before they were done. Wednesday was the school social, earlier than the others, as the students left at three. Katie met every elementary child on the island, from preschool up, and three of them were Janine's. The teachers, though? Once the children were gone, Katie was their excuse to live it up for several hours. Thursday was spent scheduling the reception tenting on the point. There were chairs to organize, locations to mark, and food! Where was the food to be served!

Then, the night before, everyone she knew started rolling in off the ferry, and that had broken into her carefully apportioned memories, and she had cried half the night.

Of course, being the night before the wedding, she hadn't stayed out at Carver Point. Preparations would be going on out there from the crack of dawn, and she would have no privacy at all. No, she and Winnie had shared the owner's suite at Briar House, and that's where they were now.

"The dress is beautiful, that I'll concede."

"*You* are beautiful." Winnie reached one arm over her head and pulled her wild mane aside to rest her face against Katie's. "If anyone says otherwise, I'll sock 'em sideways."

"Thank you, Honey. Still, can I do this?" Katie felt her eyes grow damp, and she refused to cry. No, she said to herself, looking at the woman in the mirror.

You are not allowed to cry.

"What is it?" Winnie stepped around her, dressed in a satin sheath dress that just matched Katie's blue. She had been true to her word, bringing vintage Oscars for each woman in the bridal party. What a search it'd taken, she'd exclaimed, to find coordinating ones, but her "people" had come through. Each one had to be pristine on its return, though. They were just on loan.

All the woman had matching de la Renta pumps, also temporary gifts, just for the weekend.

The flower girls? Not by Oscar, but a good miniature knock-off by a talented seamstress Winnie knew.

"I wanted to spend the week with Jeff. I wanted to look forward to today, and I've hardly seen him at all. Every day something else was planned for me to do. I'm tired, Winnie. That's all."

"I have something to cheer you up. Hold on." Winnie held up one finger, and she bobbed it a few times, like one would while training a pet. As she made her way to the door, she said it again, "Stay."

"I have no patience for surprises. And it had better not be Jeff. He cannot see me in this dress." Katie turned back to the mirror, and she flipped the veil up, only to have it fall back in her face. Once again, she felt the tears rise.

"Surprise!" Winnie pulled the door wide.

Into the room swelled eight blue beauties. Ashlynn flounced in, with her tightly curled blonde tresses highlighted by a blue bow. Winnie had managed to get matching dresses for Isabell and Lesly, the only two sisters in the group. River, with her Asian features, had a blue pillbox atop her head. Lisa touted blue-ribbon curlicues trailing down her Cher-like bounty. Kambri? She was charming with a princess crown in gold to match her wire-frame glasses. Michelle's hoops dangling from her ears more than accentuated her features, but it was Ellie that stunned the crowd. Her contemporary pageboy, her cutting-edge signature look, was lofted and fluffed into a swirling halo filled with glittering blue sequins.

Katie could no longer contain her tears.

"Oh, I have missed you so much!" She threw out her arms, wanting to draw them all in, touching hands, and leaning in to brush cheek-to-cheek. Then she saw Connie, sturdy, no-nonsense Connie, there in the door, with a black-faced tablet in her hand.

"Have you signed in today, dear? I know you're here, but Corporate only knows if you've logged in on your computer. Do you need to borrow mine?"

For a moment, Katie was unsure how to respond. Then, each of the other woman held up their company tablets, and they called out, in a random, not very organized fashion, "Or mine?" "Use mine!" "No, mine!" and on until all the tablets were right in front of her.

Katie clapped in excitement. "I love you so much. All of you. Thank you all for coming."

Winnie was behind her again, and she grabbed her shoulders and pressed her face to Katie's, whispering, "Can you do it?"

"I can do it," Katie whispered back. "Absolutely. I can do anything."

"Good girl. Let's go marry us a Jeffie."

"Woo-woo!" The rest of the wedding party began to chant and cheer. Occasionally, one called, "Jeffie!" or "Marry us a Jeffie!"

All-in-all, they were having a very good time, and they did exactly what needed to be done. They lifted Katie's spirits, and she felt, for the first time all week, really felt like she could get through this day, and at the same time, enjoy every single minute of it.

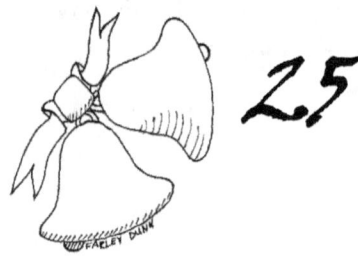

25

The small Town Church was packed. Cars went up and down the street on both sides, and inside was standing room only. Even people who didn't attend services now knew of Katie Carver, granddaughter of the Rockhaven Carvers, come back to the island to marry Jeff Ragsdale, of the Rockhaven Ragsdales.

Of course, the Rockhaven Ragsdales didn't have quite the social clout of the Carver family, but they were well-respected by the island crowd, nonetheless.

Katie's biggest surprise? Mrs. Anabelle Rosenbaum, her neighbor from Boston. It seemed Cousin Nikki and she had indeed become very good friends, and Nicolette had once again rented the longest limousine she could commandeer for the trip to the island. It created quite a stir coming off the ferry, and when word got out that it was bringing a Carver all the way from France? Katie's social standing went up another four very large notches.

Ten women wearing vintage Oscar dresses? That hardly did any damage at all. How Katie looked in her dress? Stunning. Everyone said so.

Amidst a bevy of tapers and blue and white flowers everywhere, Katie and Jeff clasped arms and knelt before God. It was when he lifted her veil and kissed her before God and everybody that she knew she was someone different. She would always be a Carver, because the Carver family tree was in her blood. Now though, she was more. She was Katie Ragsdale, the very person she'd always wanted to be.

Exiting the church, with Jeff at her side, and clapping and cheers from the attendees carrying them along, she made her way to the ridiculously enormous limousine for the ride to the Point. "You must, ma chère," Nicolette had insisted, in her fur-trimmed suit, "borrow the car. You must, you must." And she had nodded as if that were that. Once inside, the hush of the luxurious vehicle surrounded them.

"Can any day be more wonderful?" Katie pulled her veil up, attempting to find the pins in her hair to pull it loose.

"Let me help, Dame Carver." Jeff pushed her hands gently aside, and he worked the pins free, smoothing her hair as he set the veil on the seat. "There. All beautiful."

"You're wrong." Katie smirked at him. "You're very wrong."

"You are beautiful. No one can say otherwise." He

179

leaned to kiss her on the top of her head. "I have declared it, and it shall always be so."

"Not about that." Katie snuggled against him.

"What, then?" He wrapped one arm around her, pulling her in.

"I'm no longer Dame Carver. I'm Dame Ragsdale, now." She held up her hand to display her sparkling diamond ring.

"Ah, that's where we differ in opinion. Dame Ragsdale you may very well be, and I'm glad for it, but you will always be Dame Carver to me."

Katie picked up his hand and pressed the backside to her lips, kissing it gently before letting it fall back into his lap.

"What?" Jeff squeezed her shoulder. "Nothing to say?"

"Everything to say. But I can't say it all." Reaching to the door, she pulled out a tissue and held it to her eyes, pressing carefully to avoid smudging her makeup. "I can't cry, not now. Not with nearly two hundred people meeting us at the reception. What would they say?"

"That we love each other very much, I think."

"Okay." Katie took a very deep breath. "I know how to tell you everything I want to say."

"Oh?" Jeff chuckled. "It's only a twenty-minute ride. Are you sure?"

"Absolutely." Katie turned to look him in the eyes. "It's only three words."

"You can say everything you want to say to me in three words?" He laughed. "Okay."

"I love you."

"Wow," he said. "I can do better. I can say it without any words."

Without anything else said, he pulled her to him and kissed her on the lips. When he was finished, he looked at her and raised one eyebrow.

Katie leaned against him with a smile.

"How'd I do?"

"You win," she said, pulling his hand up and kissing it again. "Dame Carver is who I am forever and ever. However, I'm signing my name Katie Ragsdale."

"I should hope so. After all, you are my wife."

It was the kiss he got in return that told what she thought of that. It was exactly who she'd wanted to be her entire life.

www.ingramcontent.com/pod-product-compliance
Lightning Source LLC
Chambersburg PA
CBHW070933250626
47159CB00009B/3224